PARTNERS: BAGELS AND BEER
THE BEGINNINGS

Harrison Black

Author's Tranquility Press
Marietta, Georgia

Copyright © 2021 by Harrison Black.

All rights reserved. No part of this publication may be reproduced, distributed or transmitted in any form or by any means, including photocopying, recording, or other electronic or mechanical methods, without the prior written permission of the publisher, except in the case of brief quotations embodied in critical reviews and certain other noncommercial uses permitted by copyright law. For permission requests, write to the publisher, addressed "Attention: Permissions Coordinator," at the address below.

Harrison Black/Author's Tranquility Press
2706 Station Club Drive SW
Marietta, GA 30060
www.authorstranquilitypress.com

Publisher's Note: This is a work of fiction. Names, characters, places, and incidents are a product of the author's imagination. Locales and public names are sometimes used for atmospheric purposes. Any resemblance to actual people, living or dead, or to businesses, companies, events, institutions, or locales is completely coincidental.

Ordering Information:
Quantity sales. Special discounts are available on quantity purchases by corporations, associations, and others. For details, contact the "Special Sales Department" at the address above.

PARTNERS: BAGELS AND BEER/ Harrison Black
Paperback: 978-1-956480-66-5
eBook: 978-1-956480-67-2

Nothing frightens bad men as much as good men willing to stand in their way

Table of Contents

Canarsie Joe's Gym..7
345 88^(TH) Rooad, Woodhaven, Queens........................11
Bedford Avenue, Brooklyn 14
Manhattan Civic Center...16
NYPD Police Academy-Second Month of Training 19
NYPD Police Academy-Fifth Month of Training Cycle 24
NYPD-Rodman's Neck Firing Range 31
Police Academy Graduation Day 35
14th Precinct-Manhattan 38
The Red Feather Tavern, Manhattan..........................46
10AM on E.57th Street..48
14th Precinct – Midnight to Eight Shift.......................51
Opportunity..54
Randall's Island 56
The Grand Concourse and Marcy Place.....................58
The Next Day – Police Headquarters..........................64
102nd Detective Squad, Queens 69
The Ride..79
Homicide Case 85
New York State Supreme Court-Country of Queens.................95
NY State Offices, Queens Boulevard 104
102nd Squad...108
102nd Squad...111
The Conolly Case..115
Cammerata Case 119
Conolly Case...124
Cammarata Case 134

Conolly Case	140
Cammareta Case	145
Conolly Case	147
Cammerata Case	150
Cammerata Case	161
Conolly Case	165
Cammerata Case	168
Conolly Case	172
The Lou Monthly Meeting	175
Conolly Case	180
The Cammerata Case	188
Conolly Case	192
Cammeratta Case	195
Conolly Case	199
Cammaratta Case	205
Conolly Case	210
Cammaratta Case	213
Conolly Case	218
Conolly Case	224
Conolly Case	230
102ND Squad	232
Detective Partners	235
Homicide Case	241
Rushmore Case	247
Rushmore Case	250
Rushmore Case	257
Rushmore Case	261
Steven Witt	266
Café Odessa, Brighton Beach	271

Four Days after Dynex Heist 274
VBS Television Company, Dover, Delaware 279
102nd Squad 284
Witt Estate, Great Neck, NY 288
Fresh Meadows, Queens 292
102nd Squad 296
Café Odessa 301
Outside the East New York Distribution Associates Warehouse
.... 305
102nd Squad 310
102nd Squad 317
102nd Squad 322
Café Odessa 327
Diamond Heist 329
102nd Squad 335

CHAPTER ONE

Canarsie Joe's Gym
Brooklyn, NY
1958

The bell rang for the two-minute spar to begin. Both boxers moved toward the center of the ring. Touching gloves, they moved apart to try and defeat the defense of the other. Morris "Red" Blackman stood almost 6 feet tall and weighed in at 165. His opponent was 6'4" and weighed 200. The old trainer wanted to see how Red did against bigger opponents. The big guy threw a left jab and caught Red in his right eye; it staggered him and he brushed it off with his glove. The trainer watched and saw how Red reacted. He saw Red regain his composure, shrugged his shoulders and advanced towards his opponent with a right jab to the chest. This was so forceful and direct it rocked the opponent. He then delivered three devastating jabs to the stomach causing him to bend. The coup d'état was a left uppercut to the jaw. The larger man fell to the canvas and was out. Red went to the neutral corner and waited while the trainer tended to the downed fighter. He looked at Red and said,

"Hit the shower Red, he's had enough."

As he walked toward the showers, he remembered how far he had progressed from that day he was stopped in the street and beaten up by a neighborhood gang intent on getting a Jewish kid. The next day he walked into Carnarsie Joe's and started to learn how to defend himself. After many hard and painful days, he improved, and soon became a forced to be reckoned with. Then he panicked, looked at his watch and realized he had to rush home, for it was first night of Passover.

The rest of the Blackman family was already seated at table. Grandfather Isaac who in 1903 arrived from Russia and set up a junkyard business in 1910. Married a beautiful girl named Rachel, had 2 sons and 2 daughters, now living with his oldest son Jacob. Jacob Blackman owned a card and stationery store, army veteran of World War Two, a Ranger in the Normandy invasion who came back a captain. Jacob married Eileen Schwartzburg and had twins Robby and Amy followed by a red-headed boy Morris. Robby was his final year of surgical residency at Columbia Presbyterian Hospital, while Amy, a Princeton grad had completed the Wharton School and was now with a company called IBM. As Eileen came out of the kitchen with a platter of chicken, Jacob motioned her to sit down for the seder was to begin. As her husband began the service reading, she looked over to the empty chair. They all heard the door open and in rushed a disheveled looking Morris. His mother stood up and saw how his right eye was swollen.

"What happened to my baby?"

"Nothing ma, I'm alright." as she kissed his wound.

The twins smirked at each other and rolled their eyes. Morris sat down between his grandfather and brother. His grandfather whispered,

"What happened, you led with your eye?"

"Papa, the other guy never got a chance to hit me again."

Isaac smiled and looked to his son at the head of the table, their eyes meeting each other and there was a grin on Jacob's face. He continued with the words of the service. Since Morris was the youngest for the past 16 years, he had asked the Four Questions, so in his twentieth year he thought it was time for his brother or sister to get married and produce a replacement. He knew he was the one his parents worried about, because he had not decided on what he wanted to do. He would not work in his father's store, and though the twins were well on their way to success, he remained idle. Now in his second year at Brooklyn College majoring in English he still could not find the sign to a satisfactory life's path.

CHAPTER TWO

345 88ᵀᴴ Rooad, Woodhaven, Queens
1958

As Timothy Feeney, an engineer with the Long Island Railroad entered his home, he was greeted by his seven-year-old daughter Bridget. Entering the kitchen, he kissed his wife Laura and hugged his oldest daughter, Christine. He washed up for dinner and grabbed a beer from the refrigerator. Sitting down at the head of the table, Laura called upstairs for the boys to come down. The sound of running feet could be heard as Brendan and Philip came down. The front door opened and in walked the oldest, Sean. He nodded to his father, kissed his mother and picked up Bridget.

"So how was work today, Sean?" asked Tim.

"Mr. Collins is selling the foundry. They will be closing in six months."

Christine said, "That means you will be out work, unless you can find something else."

"Sure, looks that way. Been there since I was sixteen, got myself up to lead welder, and now the bottom drops out."

Tim interjected, "Let me ask around, maybe there is something with the railroad."

"Thanks Pop, but that is not for me. I am going to have to find a new career, and if that doesn't pan out there is always the service."

"You are not going into the service period," said his mother.

"Did you tell your girlfriend?" asked Christine.

"No, the family is the first to know, I'll tell her tomorrow."

Sean Feeney, age 20 was a handsome man at 6 feet tall and 170 pounds. His mother said he was the spitting image of her Uncle Martin Sullivan. It was said Uncle Martin had been a bookie in Brooklyn and had made a lot of money. Never married, he skirted the law and died a peaceful death at age 77. His money was divided up between Sean's mother and her sister Aunt Maggie. Aunt Maggie left for California, while Laura purchased the house they all lived in. Sean graduated from Archbishop Molloy High School and never wanted to attend college. He yearned to leave Queens and join the Marine Corps, but he had found a trade and became a craftsman, so he stayed. After dinner he went to the neighborhood bar, Crosby's. He met his two best friends, Stevie Cochran and Joe Butler. Over a round of beers, Stevie announced he was joining the Navy, while Joe was going to take the New York Police Department entrance test. Joe was sold on the benefits, and the fact that in twenty years he could retire with a great pension. The Marine Corps would have to wait. Sean asked Joe about the entrance test and when the next was scheduled. Sean could now see his future.

CHAPTER THREE

Bedford Avenue, Brooklyn
1958

Junior Morris Blackman left the campus of Brooklyn College during a break between classes. He was heading to a sandwich shop he liked when he heard the terrifying scream coming down the avenue. He looked up to see thick smoke and flames coming from a third story apartment. As people gathered, he saw a woman in the window screaming as smoke was coming out of the window next to her. People were yelling at her not to jump, but you could see she was in full panic mode. Sirens were heard, but instead of fire trucks, a single NYPD green and white patrol car pulled up. Two cops jumped out and immediately ran into the building. Morris watched as one of the officers came behind the lady in the window and grabbed her. The smoke was getting thicker, when he saw the other cop come to the window with a baby in his arms. The cop yelled toward the street crowd for help. Morris takes off and runs to front of the building directly under window.

"Can you catch her? I'll throw her down to you!"

Morris yells up,

"Go ahead, I'm ready!"

The cop lets the baby drop two floors and Morris makes a perfect catch. The flames inside the room are roaring towards the open window, when the cop leaps out. He hits an opened awning which broke the force of the fall, but the cop is lying on the sidewalk not moving. His partner with the baby's mother came over to Morris he handed the baby over to the tearful mother. He and the partner go over to the fallen cop to see if he still alive. The fire department and ambulance arrive, and Morris moves aside so they can tend to the hero officer. He watches the partner holding the fallen cops hand talking loudly,

"Davey Boy! Davey Boy hang in there, you're going to make it!"

A Police Sergeant came over and grabbed the partner so the Medics could lift him onto the stretcher. As the stretcher went past Morris saw the officer's nameplate, it said D. Silverman. Leaving the fire scene Morris is happy the baby survived, but is more concerned about the cop. In all his years he never heard of a Jewish cop. This guy was some hero, he risked his life and performed something truly awesome. It was at that moment Morris "Red" Blackman. decided to be a policeman.

CHAPTER FOUR

Manhattan Civic Center
1959

Over 4500 people showed up for the NYPD entrance exam. Morris Blackman and Sean Feeney were there to try and qualify for the 550 openings. All the applicants were seated at desks, given a pencil and a sealed test packet, and told to wait for the bell. The guy next to Sean opened his packet and before he could look at it a cop came over grabbed his pencil, took the packet and escorted him out from the auditorium. It was about a three-minute wait before the bell sounded. The applicants had 2 hours to complete the test. Morris was on the west side of the auditorium. He read every question slowly and answered all the questions, he finished in fifty minutes. Raising his hand, a uniformed came over and collected it. He was told he could leave the auditorium. Sean took an hour and fifteen minutes and as he exited the building, he hoped e qualified.

Three months from the date of the test both men received notice that they had qualified. Morris was listed as number 15 and Sean was number 64. They were advised to report to the Police Academy in three weeks at 0800 hours sharp and start training as Class #732.

Three weeks later Morris walks into the Police Academy Auditorium at 0730 hours and took a seat near the front. Sean walked in at 0745 hours and took a seat in the eighth row. Other persons were arriving and soon the room began to fill up. At exactly 0800 hours a uniformed lieutenant came up to the front podium and began to speak.

"Welcome Class #732 to the NYPD. Today you begin your training to become a person worthy to wear our uniform. You have qualified for the best and biggest Police Department in the country by passing the entry exam. We here will provide you with the best training in law enforcement, and each of you will implement that training on the street. This job is not an easy line of work. It is highly dangerous, deadly, tragic yet personally rewarding, interesting and sometimes very humorous. We are a para-military organization that runs like a clock. Each of you will be trained in making decisions, some good and some bad. Hopefully this training will alleviate the negative and prove the positive. You will be carrying a loaded weapon 24 hours a day; never underestimate the responsibility this incurs. I want you to look at the guy on your left and the guy on your right. Today, there are 550 of you, in six months that number will dwindle, and that man on either side of you may not be here to graduate."

He stopped speaking because five people had arrived late. They each had to find a seat and that took a few minutes. The lieutenant waited for them to be seated. He motioned to several officers in the room to stand by. His next words stunned everyone.

"The five people who came in late, please stand up."

They all stood up.

"You were told to be here at 0800 hours sharp. You did not comply with that order. Gentlemen you are dismissed from this class. Try next year and be on time. Officers escort these people off the premises."

Morris watched as one of the five walked by crying.

"Now there are 545 of you to start training. There is no being late here. Orders are to be followed

and regulations are to be adhered to, for you are no longer in a democracy to choose what and when you do things. Get used to it and get used to it fast. Welcome Class # 732 and the best of luck."

CHAPTER FIVE

NYPD Police Academy-Second Month of Training
1959

Criminal Law class started every day at 0800 hours and finished 1200 hours. This was an intense class with a lot of bookwork and memorization. The class had been reduced to 525 as the first month of physical conditioning had caused some resignations. Everyone and everything were constantly evaluated. Morris has risen from 15th to 10th, while Sean had fallen from 64th to 75th in the class standings. In law class the trainees were peppered with questions and situations. Those that were deemed exceptional in this phase were advanced to special status as team instructors. Morris was designated an instructor and soon had a group of trainees to prep and get them up to baseline. At 1315 hours each day they met in small classrooms. In the group were Sullivan, McCarthy, Feeney, McBride, Shea, Tozzi and Robinson. Today they would discuss misdemeanors and Morris used shoplifting as an example. Immediately McCarthy interrupted and said,

"Robinson should know all about this one, his people do a lot of it."

McBride and Sullivan laughed, while Robinson who was black sat and remained silent.

"Why would you say that McCarthy? This is a criminal offense of the law, not a perception of a group." said Morris.

"Because they all steal and that is a fact."

Robinson immediately stood up to face the bigot.

"Sit down Sambo, or I will knock you down!"

Morris said,

"McCarthy that was not necessary. We are here to learn this course and get each of you up to baseline. Do you understand?"

"Yeah, but I don't need to hear that from a god damn kike!"

McCarthy was the biggest man in the class. He stood at 6'5" and was at least 230 lbs. He looked at his buddies McBride, Sullivan and Shea who all replied with a right on.

Sean remained quiet. There was a silence that filled the room then Morris spoke.

"This session is over; we meet again same time tomorrow. McCarthy, will you accompany me to the gym for some boxing? Let's see if you can beat a god damn kike."

McCarthy got red in the face, he got up and looked to his Irish buddies to back him up. McBride, Sullivan and Shea got up to follow. McCarthy looked at Sean and said.

"What's the matter with you Feeney, you're not backing us?"

"Not today, I'm backing the Jewish guy, he's smarter."

Robinson said,

"I'll be behind you Blackman against this jerk."

Tozzi looked at McCarthy and his buddies and said,

"I'll make sure it stays one against one."

They all left for the gym. In a few minutes word had spread that two guys from the class were going to box. By the time both parties were getting their gloves tied on, a crowd including several instructors had gathered. As both men circled the mat, most of the noise came from the McCarthy side.

Morris moved in closer, McCarthy swung a huge right at his head. He easily ducked under and delivered two stiff blows to McCarthy's stomach. He continued to bob and move to McCarthy's right, several right jabs that connected with McCarthy's nose. The nose started to bleed, McCarthy was enraged and started swinging roundhouse punches that connected with air. Morris again moved in closer, changed his stance and connected three times with his left to McCarthy's head. He hit him in both eyes and stunned the larger man. McCarthy was not a fighter just a large man with brawn. He looked scared as he looked to his friends. McBride and Shea moved around the mat to be behind Morris, so as to set him up for their buddy. Robinson moved quickly and hit McBride in the jaw so hard he dropped to the floor. Shea was ready to move when Sean tapped him on the shoulder and dropped him to the floor. Tozzi slowly walked over to Sullivan and said,

"Not a good idea, don't you agree?"

Sullivan remained in place and said nothing.

McCarthy expecting some support was all alone and was getting the shit kicked out of him. As Morris continued to circle, McCarthy never saw the multiple shots to his body and head. He went down hard and was breathing heavily on the mat. Sean came over and leaned over and said,

"You get up and fight you dumb mick because I am going to hurt you more, or you publicly apologize to Robinson then to me. Your choice asshole!"

McCarthy was in a lot of pain; he chose to save his skin.

"Robinson, I am sorry what I said about your people I was wrong. Blackman no more I'm done.

I apologize for calling you a kike, I'm sorry".

It took him over ten minutes to get up from the mat. His buddies were nowhere to be seen. The head Academy instructor Deputy Inspector Averill had been watching. He came over to Morris.

"You know you could be thrown out for that, but I understand what happened. Some advice, use this moment to your advantage. You have achieved the respect of the class and staff, keep it that way."

Morris smiled and said,

"Yes Sir."

Sean, Robinson and Tozzi came over. Morris said,

"Thanks for the backup, guys, much appreciated."

Sean replied,

"Now what were you saying about shoplifting?"

They all laughed and walked out of gym together.

CHAPTER SIX

NYPD Police Academy-Fifth Month of Training Cycle
1960

The week after the New Year the class had been reduced 480 due to academic failures. Morris was now rated eighth, while Sean made a turn around and was rated thirty-second. Both Morris and Sean had become friends by this time, and were off hours drinking buddies. Crime Scene investigation was this week's subject matter. The trainees would be introduced to various crime scenes and learn about preserving evidence. Every day a different detective came and gave a talk. These were the best investigators in the department, and they got everyone's attention. Burglary was defined as a victimless crime, but the actions of the thief in penetrating a person's private sanctum could terrorize the victim. It was stressed that the responding officers secure the scene, keep the victim safe and away from the point of entry. Being able to determine the entry point was important for the incoming investigators. A street assault scene first needed to be secured. It was critical to determine if the victim required medical care. All witnesses needed to be questioned and identified to give the responding investigators a clearer picture. Robberies were discussed in full, and what the street officer duties were especially to those victims who were in direct contact. A FDNY Fire Marshal spoke about Arson cases, while a Detective gave a great presentation on pickpockets and confidence scams. A Detective Captain from the Crime Lab explained the workings of his group and described the cases that were solved by collecting the smallest of evidence. The counterfeiting of currency was given by a United States Secret Service Agent who passed around counterfeit bills for everyone to see and feel. A team of detectives from the Bomb Squad and an ATF agent kept everyone on edge with how to make a bomb and the signature of the bomb makers. All in all, everyone agreed this week was one of the best, but the next subject Homicide was what Sean and Morris were waiting for. Detective Captain Peter Longstreet was a legend in the NYPD. He entered wearing a three-piece suit and looking like a Wall Street banker. He was just under 6' tall and maybe a thin 160 pounds. He exuded a sense of importance and character. His brown hair was speckled with gray and his green eyes very piercing. In a clear voice he started.

"Gentlemen, Homicide is a crime of extreme violence, sometimes planned, sometimes done in a millisecond, and sometimes accidental. Anything can be a weapon from a high-powered rifle to a butter knife. You will be the first persons responding and you will have to remember these basics;

1. Enter the scene slowly using all your senses. What's the first thing you see, hear, smell feel?

2. Determine if you are in danger. Is the perpetrator still present? Have they left the scene?

3. Do not touch or move the victim. Listen if they are breathing, look for a rise and fall in the chest area. If you see breathing call for medical, if not call your supervisor to come to the scene.

4. First do a quick check around the body. Evidence such as blood, a weapon, a spent shell casing, etc. may be present, but do not touch or remove anything, just note the location.

5. You and your partner must guard the entrance and await the arrival of the investigatory personnel. Record the name and times of their arrival. They now have authority of the crime scene.

6. Away from the body do a quick search of the immediate premises looking for points of entry, points of departure, additional blood evidence, the murder weapon, bullet holes in the walls, etc.

7. Keep victim's family or relationships away from the crime scene and isolated. Await the investigators.

8. Look for and identify things that were on such as radios and televisions. Was the stove on and what was in it? Was the water running? Is there animal food or a dish on the floor? If so where is the animal?

9. When the investigators arrive, record their entry and name, and brief them on what you found. Everything you have observed is important.

10. Since you and your partner were the first ones to respond, you will be the last ones to leave. You record the times all personnel leave, especially when the body of the victim is removed from the premises. You wait until your Sergeant puts up the crime scene tape and notice. Then you can leave the crime scene.

11. You will probably be ordered by the investigating detectives to canvass the building, neighborhood, etc. to determine if someone saw or heard something. If you find a credible witness with information, immediately notify the Detective in charge of the case.

That is what you do as the responding uniformed officer, now my job begins. If we retrieve good evidence and get good leads, we will find the perpetrator within 48 hours. If we have no leads and the physical evidence is sketchy, we will have a more complex investigation. Every aspect of evidence be it actual or forensic determined must be tracked down. All human relationships must be investigated from a grieving mother to a witness passing by. It is a game of gathering the dots then connecting them together. When you have a suspect, he or she will have to be surveilled. How much time and manpower can we spend on this? Does this case require electronic surveillance and special warrants? Most important is the victim. Was the victim an innocent person or a perpetrator with a record? In the case of an innocent there may be more than meets the eye. The weapon used to commit the crime, was it retrieved and was it used in a previous homicide? The type of weapon used can give insight into the killer and their psyche. These are just a few aspects of the Homicide Investigation needed to bring to justice the perpetrator. Thank you and best of luck to each of you in your police career."

As Longstreet left the podium, most of the class was filing out of the auditorium except Morris and Sean. They had been taken by this lecture and needed to ask questions.

Morris said,

"Excuse me Detective Longstreet my name is trainee Morris Blackman. May I ask you a question?"

"Sure, go ahead."

"How did you become a Detective?"

Longstreet thought for a second to frame his response.

"The answer to that is not readily discussed here and in the department. There are three ways.

First, you have a name that is related to someone in a powerful department position. My experience has shown these individuals are useless and not intelligent. Second, as a patrolman. you make a lot of good collars. This means all your arrests go to court and hold up. Sooner or later the suits upstairs have to make you a Detective 3rd grade because you have earned it.

And lastly the fastest way to a Detective shield is to make an arrest that produces great media exposure, such as arresting the kidnapper of a child, rescuing and innocent from a deadly situation, or arresting a high-profile criminal on the loose. That is how you become a detective."

"I'm trainee Sean Feeney. What collar got you the Detective shield?"

"Working in the 5-7th Brooklyn, I was a beat cop. I'm walking the main avenue in Bed-Stuy when I hear shots fired. Right above me a guy with a rifle is picking off people. I see about four persons lying in the street and on the sidewalk. We did not have radios then just a box key, and the closest box would have exposed me to the gunman. I found the entrance to the building that the shooter was in, entered and went up the stairs to the first floor with my revolver drawn. I could hear more shots fired but they were coming from the next floor up. By this time, he had shot about seven times. I went up to the second floor, and heard more shots coming from another floor above. Thank God it was only a three-floor building. On the third floor I had to check about six apartments. You had to listen for any movement, then four more shots were heard from the last apartment on the floor. I slowly tried the doorknob and it moved. Knowing the shooter was inside and was about to shoot more people, it was pretty clear what I had to do. Revolver fully forward I went in slowly and quietly hugged the wall. I heard sounds from the room facing the street of metal against metal, he was reloading the rifle. I ran into the room and saw him on the floor, he looked at me and moved the rifle toward me. I fired into him six times. The killing shot was to the head, followed by 2 to his chest. I dropped to the floor, and that is where they found me. He had killed eight innocent people and wounded six. I became a hero cop with my face on every front page. The perp I killed was an ex-con on parole who came back to his neighborhood to settle some scores. I got a medal from the Department and was made a 3rd Grade Detective. Next thing I know I'm out of Brooklyn and working with the 17th Squad in Manhattan. Today, I command four squads of Homicide detectives for Manhattan South. Look guys, I have a meeting in thirty minutes, I hope I answered your questions. Good luck to both of you."

As he left both of them looked at each other and at the same time said,

"I am going to be a Detective."

CHAPTER SEVEN

NYPD-Rodman's Neck Firing Range
1960

Rodman's Neck is located in the Bronx. The NYPD conducts all firearms training here for it offers a safe and secluded area on a peninsula facing Long Island Sound. With large earthen berms on the beach, all trainees are brought here to learn how to fire a firearm. At this juncture in time, Class # 732 now numbered 467. Notable of the losses were trainees McCarthy and Sullivan. On a weekend they got drunk and were stopped on the Belt Parkway. Their alcohol and blood levels were way over the legal limit. Both were dismissed from the Academy and prosecuted as civilians. Those remaining were told that the firearms training course required a score of 290 to pass. The final in four weeks would be a timed fifty shot event using the service weapon they were assigned.

The test would include shooting from different positions which included behind barricades, sitting, prone and walking toward a target. For the next four weeks they would be able to practice and refine their shooting skills until the test week on week four. Safety was the key issue stressed, and anyone not adhering to the basic range rules and voice commands would be dismissed immediately. The first week was all classroom learning how to assemble and disassemble their weapon, how to clean it, bullet ballistics, and most important when to draw your weapon. Second week was weapon familiarization and firing. Morris was in the second group and took his position. Over the range loudspeaker came the order to present their weapons. The service weapon was a six-inch .38 Special caliber called the Smith and Wesson Model 10. Told to load six rounds, each trainee loaded six .38 special bullets into the cylinder. Morris closed the cylinder and kept the pistol pointed downrange. He awaited the order to fire. At least thirty seconds passed when the order came to open fire. Morris took aim and squeezed the trigger. He fired and to his amazement he expected more of a retort. He fired off the next five rounds, opened the cylinder ejected the shells and waited for a range safety officer to see his empty cylinder. The officer came by and said,

"Clear, you can re-holster your weapon."

He waited for the last person in the group to be cleared, then they were ordered to retrieve their targets. As he walked the twenty-five yards to his target, he saw no holes. Removing the target from the holder he walked back to his firing position. There was one hole in the paper well below the target rings. An instructor came by and said,

"First time you ever fired a gun?"

"Yes Sir."

"Well you are jerking the trigger, not squeezing it slowly. It is throwing all your shots to the bottom. Raise your front sight to sit just below the bottom ring."

"Yes Sir, will do."

The next round of six, Morris put three to top of the bottom ring.

Sean who had never shot a gun before was a natural. Using what he learned in the classroom he took his time, framed the shot in his mind, and slowly squeezed the trigger. All of his first six shots were within the rings and one just below the bullseye.

"Well now what do we have here a real Hopalong Cassidy? Keep it up you're doing fine."

A beaming Feeney responded,

"Yes Sir."

Three weeks later the final and qualifying shoot was upon class #732. Morris was in third group he was anxious to qualify on the first round. The timed event was ten minutes long and the trainee had to complete firing fifty shots from fifty yards out. A minimum score of 290 was required to pass. Each trainee had three rounds to qualify. Morris's fifty shots took him seven minutes to complete and his final score was 325. He had passed and was one of the early leaders on the board. Sean shot in the last group of the day. He completed it in four minutes and 10 seconds scoring 490 out of a possible 500 points. The instructors told him he had broken the range record for trainees by 35 points.

With only one week left of Academy training Morris was rated number one in the class and Sean, with his unique shooting ability had now risen to number 14.

CHAPTER EIGHT

Police Academy Graduation Day
Class #732
1960

They were dressed in their new blue uniforms and caps. Today was the day they would join the Finest. Family and friends filled Madison Square Garden as the 475 proud marched into the arena and were seated. As the speakers finished, the class was getting anxious for they wanted the badge they had each earned, and their destination orders to their new precinct.

Morris Blackman was the first name called. As he got and walked to the stage, he saw his proud and smiling mother and father. At the podium he was given his badge and an envelope. The department Chief of Personnel, Chief Haggerty, told him to remain. Haggerty spoke to the audience.

"Ladies and Gentlemen, it gives me great pleasure to introduce our Class honor graduate Morris Blackman. Officer Blackman achieved a cumulative score of 97.5 during his training cycle. Your name will be the Academy Honor Roll that is on display at the Academy. In addition, you have earned the Officer William Todd Memorial Award recognizing you as the top honor graduate." He handed Morris a small package and shook his hand. To the noise of applause Morris saluted and proceeded off the stage. The 14th name read was Sean Feeney, and a roar came from the audience. It appeared the entire family Feeney was present. He was given his badge and an envelope, and Chief Haggerty again came forward.

"Ladies and Gentlemen, we are proud to announce that Officer Feeney was our finest marksman. He broke the scoring record that has stood for 16 years. It is my honor to present you with the Sgt. Otto Werner Memorial Award for marksmanship." He presented Sean with a small package and as he left the stage, he spotted his father smiling, and sister Bridget jumping up and down.

Class number 38 belonged to Ed Tozzi and number 45 to William Washington. After the last man was called to the stage the class stood in unison and applauded him. With their badges pinned to their uniform they stood at attention and raised their right hands for the oath. Each of the 475 were very proud of their accomplishment and looking forward to "working the job".

The four friends got together and hugged each other. As agreed upon they would now open their envelopes and find out where they would be going. Tozzi got the six-three in Brooklyn, Washington the one-o-one in Queens. Sean opened his and found he was going to the one-seven in Manhattan while Morris got the one-four also in Manhattan. They all agreed to keep in touch and wished each other the best of success. Each hoped that someday they would run into each other, but now each had to face his own assignment and future.

CHAPTER NINE

14th Precinct-Manhattan
1960

Officer Morris Blackman, Badge #36782 reported for shift muster in the ready room.

Sgt. Tom Mann was the supervisor of the shift and he called the muster to order. He called out names and assigned them sectors. Morris was called last.

"You're on probation Blackman, so you will be assigned with a senior officer. He would be with Officer Rocco Navarro, a beat man at Herald Square. As they walked out of the precinct Navarro looked at Morris and said,

"What's your name kid?"

"Morris Blackman"

"I'm not going to remember that. I'll call you Red, is that ok?"

"Yeah ok."

Said Morris, thinking how hard it is to remember Blackman.

"Well Red, you follow me today and do not do anything unless I tell you do it, got that?"

"Yes, Sir."

They walked the six blocks over to Herald Square and stood outside Macy's on 34th Street.

In about twenty minutes Navarro looked at his watch and said,

"Should be right about now."

"What?" asked Red.

"The money pick-up."

Just then a Brinks armored truck pulled right up to the curb where they were standing and two

armed guards got out. Exchanging hellos with Navarro they went to the back of the truck, knocked and the door opened. A heavy-duty hand truck appeared and then boxes of coins were passed out and stacked. After some twenty boxes were stacked. The door was swung shut and the guards wheeled it into the store.

"We wait here for them to come back out. Get your hand away from your gun!"

"Sorry."

In about ten minutes he saw the guards pushing the hand truck this time stacked with four large canvas money bags. As they reached the street, they knocked on the rear door and it opened.

Loading the four bags into the truck, they shut the door. One of the guards gave a wave to Navarro and the truck took off. Navarro again looked at his watch and motioned for Red to follow. They walked across Broadway and Seventh Avenue to the northeast corner.

"Wait here."

Navarro and Red stood there for fifteen minutes. Red saw a patrol car approaching, as it got closer, he saw it was Sgt. Mann and his driver. The car stopped in front of them, Mann rolled down the window and said,

"How's it going Rocco?"

"Everything is alright Sarge"

With that he rolled up the window and went across 34th Street.

Navarro said,

"Ok, were finished here follow me."

He crossed 34th Street and entered the Hotel McGlennon. Walking past the front desk he went over to the elevators. One arrived and they both entered. Navarro pulled out a key from his pocket and inserted it in the control panel. He turned the key and pressed a button marked SB.

The elevator went down and opened on a dark floor. Navarro stepped out and pushed a light switch and the floor was lit. Red saw a sign that said Sub-Basement. Navarro then opened a door that lead into a room. Putting on the light Red saw a cot, a table, and a chair. Navarro took off his gun belt and laid down on the cot, he motioned Red to sit in the chair.

"What are we doing now?"

"Well I am going to take a nap here for the next six hours, then slowly walk back to the precinct for end of shift. Make yourself comfortable."

"But what about the Sergeant? He will be looking for us."

"He already saw us, he's not coming back."

"We can be fired for this; I don't think this is a good idea Officer Navarro."

"Relax kid, you're with me and nobody touches me, I got myself a Rabbi."

"You're Jewish?"

"No stupid, not that kind of Rabbi. My Rabbi has pull within the department, he protects me.

"Who is your Rabbi?"

"My brother-in-law is Pete Farrentino."

"Is he a Captain?"

"Bigger than that, he is the President of the Columbia Association, 6800 members and they all vote."

Red was astounded, he looked at Navarro who was nodding off. His first day on the job and he is being taught Corruption 101. Maybe it will be better the next day.

Two weeks later during the 4-12 shift of the 17th Precinct.

Sean Feeney is walking a regular beat alone. Third Avenue from E.41st to E.43rd streets is his assigned area, and he is getting to know the neighborhoods. He is walking up the avenue when he notices several street vendors selling their wares from blankets on the sidewalk. He sees the items are perfumes, knock off handbags, and shirts. These guys have taken up residence right in front of several stores. He decides to approach and check licenses. One of the vendors a tall black man dressed in colorful native garb is trying to sell a handbag to a lady passing by. She stops and looks at the bag, she holds the bag and then she and vendor are arguing over the price. She sees Sean and drops the bag down onto the blanket and walks away. The vendor sees Sean and says,

"What do you want?"

"I want to see your street vendor license."

"I left it home."

"Then show me a driver's license or some other picture ID."

"I left that home also."

"Ok you have twenty minutes to pick up your stuff and leave this location, your violating city ordinances. I'll give you a break, when I come back you better be gone, or I will issue a summons."

"Ok officer, I understand."

Sean moved out and continued his foot patrol. Twenty minutes later he is again walking up the avenue and sees the same vendor doing business. Sean walks up to him taps him on the back with his night stick. The vendor turns around and does not look surprised that Sean is going to give him a summons. He looks at Sean and says,

"Hey Officer, can we speak over here?"

Sean follows him to a darkened storefront. The vendor reaches into his pocket and pulls out a wad of cash.

"How much do you want to leave me and my business alone? $400 or $600?"

"Are you trying to bribe me?"

"Call it what you want, I just want you out of here so I can make some money."

Sean reached for his handcuffs and swung the vendor around.

"You're under arrest for attempting to bribe a police officer."

He then affixes both cuffs and turns the prisoner back around. He is now confronted with some ten street persons yelling,

"Let him go! Let him go! Let him go!

More people arrive and Sean and his prisoner are stuck in the storefront.

He cannot move, so he holds his prisoner with one hand while his other is on his gun.

A traffic cop in the middle of the avenue notices the commotion and runs to the corner call

box to report an officer in trouble. Within a minute, sirens are heard, and five patrol cars show up at the scene The Sergeant gets out and tell his men to disperse the crowd. He comes over to Sean and asks,

"Feeney what is this all about?"

"He has no peddler license, I told him to move and he did not move. Then he attempted to bribe me."

"How much was he offering?"

"Four to six hundred dollars."

"You dumb bastard, why didn't you take it?"

"Because that is breaking the law!"

"Listen to me Feeney and listen good. You take them handcuffs off this guy and continue on your beat. If you press this arrest, the most he will be fined is $25 bucks. Meanwhile you will be tied up in court and that will cost the city money. These guys and corners like this can bring in a few thousand bucks a day, so what he was offering was a business expense. Sean thought for a moment then released the vendor. The vendor reached into his pocket and offered it to Sean. He refused and walked away. He did not see the Sergeant shake hands with the vendor and take the money. A block away he found a coffee shop and took a seat in the rear. The waitress brought him coffee and a menu. He sat there and went over what had just happened. What they had taught him the academy was opposite that of the street. His world for the moment was upside down, and he needed to call his friend Red.

CHAPTER TEN

The Red Feather Tavern, Manhattan
1960

Red entered the dark bar and looked to the back. He saw Sean in a single booth. This was a good place to meet because it was in a precinct they did not work in and nobody would notice.

Red says,

"Hey Monsignor Feeney smile, it can only get worse."

"I don't know what to do Red."

Sean then proceeded to tell him about the street vendor.

Red responded with his day with Navarro.

"First, do nothing. The good part is that now you know what to look for and expect, so this was a learning lesson.

"Yeah, for six months we were trained to do the opposite, now you're telling me to let it happen and learn from it?

"Exactly, be aware of it and identify the participants. Store that info way back in mind and keep it for the future. We are trying to be honest Dudley Do-rights in a job that is defined by corruption and money. In this type of system, we have no future if we speak out, but we can succeed if we concentrate on getting righteous collars and working the system."

"How do we do that?"

"We both join the PBA, you join the Hibernians, I join the Shomrim and let our names be known. Then you and I wait for something to come up where we can team up. What can be better than having each other's back. Be patient Sean, if we fight the system we lose. If we find the back door that takes us up the staircase, we can beat these bastards. Patience is the key."

"Ok buddy, one thing I can learn to be is patient. Let's hit this full speed."

"Now you're talking Monsignor Feeney."

CHAPTER ELEVEN

10AM on E.57th Street
1960

Socialite Devin Montrose, wife of real estate magnate Harry Montrose, exited her limo in front of Bergdof Goodman. It did not escape the eyes of Richie Evans, professional thief. Her purse was dangling from her right arm when Richie grabbed it and ran west on the street. Mrs. Montrose went down screaming and pointing to the fleeing thief. Sean Feeney heard the scream and saw a man running carrying a purse. He gave chase. At the corner of 6th Avenue he yelled,

"Police stop!"

Richie turned it up a notch to super-fast. Sean increased his pursuit. Moving up 6th the chase hit 59th Street, when a yellow cab brushed Richie knocking him down. Lying in the street he had hurt his left leg. Sean came up and turned him on his stomach, Richie screamed in pain. Sean cuffed him and went through his pockets he found a four-inch switchblade. The cabdriver came forth holding the purse Richie was carrying.

"Thanks. Hey, would you mind driving me and this piece of shit back to 57th and Fifth."

"No problem officer, it would be my pleasure."

At 57th and Fifth he found a patrol car team taking a report from a distraught elegant woman.

A he approached with Richie in hand, she said,

"That is my purse!"

Sean asked her,

"Ma'me is this the man who took your purse?

"It was so quick I did not see his face, but the clothes match."

"Would you be willing to sign a statement stating that?"

"Yes, I would."

"Will you please check the contents. Is anything missing?"

"Everything is here."

"We require that you come down to the precinct so we can finish up the proper paperwork, can you do that today? I would appreciate that."

"Officer what is your name?"

"Patrolman Sean Feeney, 17th Precinct."

"Well Officer Feeney I know the mayor and I will tell him how you were of great service to me."

"Well thank you Ma'me."

Sean turned to the two patrol cops and said,

"I need a lift back with my prisoner to book this guy."

In the patrol car Sean came to realize he just got his first righteous collar, and no one could take that away from him.

CHAPTER TWELVE

14th Precinct – Midnight to Eight Shift
1960

Red was on foot patrol walking down 9th Avenue between 39th and 40th Street. All the streetlights were out, and, on the sidewalks, it was pitch black, only the headlights of cars illuminated the area. He was passing an alley when he heard voices. He stopped and walked slowly into alley. The voices got louder as he proceeded farther in.

"Please I have a gold ring, take it!"

"Fuck you bitch, now lift up that skirt and let's get down to business."

"No please I'm getting married next week!"

"Shut up! I don 't give a shit, get on the ground now!"

She laid down on the ground and started crying. As he unbuckled his belt and dropped his pants he was in full erection and was smiling at his conquest.

"You stay still and let me fuck you. If you give me trouble, I will kill ya."

Just then Red lit up the scene with flashlight. In his other hand was his cocked revolver aimed at the perp.

"Hey asshole, I will put a bullet in your cock first, then in your head. Now get off of her and on your belly now."

The perp moved to right and laid on his stomach face down.

Red, came over and cuffed his hands, then went through his pockets and found a cheap revolver fully loaded.

He placed the gun in his pants pocket. He went over to the female.

"Miss are you ok?"

Crying she nodded yes.

"I'm going to help you up. Are you able to walk with me to the corner?

She nodded yes.

Red, got the perp up on his feet and they all moved down the alley to the avenue. At the corner was a call box and Red called it in requesting a Sergeant and an ambulance. He forced the perp to sit on the curb, while he went over to the victim. He made sure she was covered, and nothing was exposed. She leaned into him and started crying. The Sergeant and another patrol arrived followed by an ambulance.

He explained what he discovered and showed the gun he had taken off the perp. The Sergeant told him to turn over the perp to the patrol car, the ambulance crew loaded the victim on a stretcher destination St. Vincent's Hospital. Then the Sergeant told Red to get in his car and they would follow the ambulance. They remained and waited for the victim's examination to be over. They took her home to her apartment on W. 36th Street near 8th Avenue, then returned to the precinct. The perp was one Theo Mullins who had a long yellow sheet of street crime and assaults. With the loaded gun charge and sexual assault Theo would be taking a 7-10-year vacation. Red smiled when he left the precinct for home, this was a righteous collar and it was all his.

CHAPTER THIRTEEN

Opportunity
1961

A new Mayoral administration brought some new changes with the naming of a new Police Commissioner. It seemed he had some progressive ideas, so they were immediately implemented. The men working the streets did not see these changes until the end of January. Notices on every precinct billboard were calling for volunteers to train for a special unit devoted to Urban Law Enforcement. Applicants must be patrolman, special between five feet ten and six foot five in height, unmarried, and be ready for assignment in all boroughs. A special pay stipend of $100 extra per month was included. This drew the attention of both Red and Sean. This might be the chance for them to work together. This new program was financed by a huge Federal grant, so everyone in the NYPD was happy because it cost the taxpayer nothing. They met at the Red Feather on a Thursday night. Red was attending night classes at the John Jay College of Criminal Justice to complete his bachelor's degree. With his past credits from Brooklyn College being fully accepted, he was assured of graduation this coming spring. Sean did not seek the college degree. Instead he was heavily involved with the PBA as the assistant steward representing the 17th Precinct. He was learning the importance of understanding the labor contract between the city and the union, protecting the rights of the membership.

Red says,

"Sean if we get accepted to this program, we can finally get away from all the dirtballs and corruption."

Sean replies,

"It looks pretty good. My Sergeant says the department will be giving additional training three months prior to startup. The only thing I do not understand is why the start is in the Bronx?"

"Simple, the Bronx has the highest crime rate in all the city. This program suits the brass. If it works, they get good bang for the money and accolades from the citizenry. First, we have to get accepted. Now is the time to push some of the influence we have You use the PBA, I'll talk to the Inspector at headquarters I know from the Shomrim. He's the one who told me to take care of my degree."

"I'm with you buddy, let's get moving and see what the system can do for us.

CHAPTER FOURTEEN

Randall's Island
1961

They both reported to the new unit in late March. There were five hundred officers ready for training. The next three months they underwent more physical training than they had in the Academy. Martial Arts instructors taught them all new and intricate moves. They were given a new baton that had a handle and even a course of training called the Koga Method. They were given a new sidearm to carry, the Smith and Wesson Model 13, a .357 Magnum that could penetrate the radiator of a car. A week of firearms training and all were qualified. They were told that upon completion of the course they would be formed into teams and seconded to precincts in the Bronx. There would be five teams of 100 men equivalent to a company in the Army. The team would be divided five squads of twenty per squad. During the hours of 3PM thru 11PM squads would patrol designated trouble areas and moved around the precinct every two days. It was decided that a squad would divide into 10 two-man teams and saturate a given patrol area. Each man will have a two-way FM radio on them. Even this was an experiment to see if would be successful for future department use. They were given wide authority to "stop and frisk" individuals they believed to be suspicious. Any time they stopped an individual they would fill out a "Stop Card", submitted at end of shift and forwarded up to command. On the last day of training Red and Sean stood shoulder to shoulder and received their collar pins. The pin had three capital letters TPF, the experiment had begun and the Tactical Patrol Force was activated.

CHAPTER FIFTEEN

The Grand Concourse and Marcy Place
1961

It was a cold April morning; the teams had switched to daytime hours which was agreeable with everyone. Today they were saturating the 44th Precinct. The squad split up and Red and Sean were walking over to the Grand Concourse. They didn't talk, but their eyes and ears took in everything. They turned into Marcy Place and were nearing Sheridan Avenue. Sheridan was a commercial hub of small stores, a bank, and a large bakery. Red moved his hand and touched Sean.

"What?", said Sean.

"See that green Ford parked across from the Bank. Do you see the driver?"

"Yeah, he's behind the wheel and smoking a cigarette."

"Well why on this freaking cold day is his window fully open. Look at the pile of butts on the ground, and the plate on the car isn't a New York plate. The bank is getting hit!"

"Jesus Christ, how do want to play this?"

"You walk on the opposite side with your summons book out and hitting every meter, let him think you're a traffic cop, and be ready to come out shooting."

Sean took off his overcoat and hat put it the sidewalk.

"I going to try and make it over to that bodega across from the bank and hope he doesn't see me. Let's move!"

Sean thought he saw a smile on Red's face as they parted. Red hit the corner and walked across side by side with a rather large woman pulling a grocery cart. At the corner he turned up towards the car and steadily hugged the storefronts. He got to the bodega and found a small corner niche to remain hidden. With full view of the driver and Sean slowly moving meter to meter, he knew this would end within a minute. There was movement from the front entrance of the bank. Three men appeared with stocking masks and were carrying duffel bags moving towards the car. He heard the car start up, he yelled,

"Police stop!"

Thinking it was only one cop the driver fired from inside the car. Red shot twice thru the windshield killing the driver. Red took cover behind a parked car as the three drew weapons and fired at him. One of them had a sawed-off shotgun and took aim at Red. Sean put a .357 bullet through his head. The remaining two dropped their duffels and started shooting. Red returned fire, Sean remained standing and calmly killed one of them instantly with a bullseye shot thru his heart. The remaining gunman screamed.

"Don't shoot I give up!"

Sean had advanced and kept his gun on the perp while Red came up from behind him and forced him to the street to cuff him. People now were looking out windows at the street scene. Red got on the radio.

"TPF squad 5-5, bank robbery at Manufacturers Hanover Sheridan Avenue, 3 perps dead, one in custody, squad officers ok. Send Sergeant and ambulance. Going inside bank. Out"

Sean stayed with cuffed perp and Red went inside the bank. It was carnage. Three dead on the floor all shot in the head. He heard a voice and went over to the opened vault; a male was lying on the floor with a gaping stomach wound. Red saw a jacket hung over a chair and immediately pressed that into the wound. The male was breathing, and his eyes opened.

"Hey buddy, what's your name?"

"Roger White."

"You the bank manager?"

"Yes."

"Well Roger White, an ambulance is coming, you're going to make it, just stay still."

"How are my people?"

"They're being taken of, you don't need to worry."

Sirens were heard outside, five armed officers entered. Red yelled,

"I'm a cop, I got a live one, needs an ambulance forthwith!"

The ambulance crew came in and placed Roger on the stretcher. Red held his hand and said,

"You're going to live Roger do not give up."

Outside he saw Sean and went over and hugged him.

"Thanks, that dirtbag with the shotgun had me in his sights."

"Well we cannot break up this friendship like that."

They both laughed. Around them it looked like the entire Police world had converged upon them.

Sean had put the handcuffed robber into a patrol car. Now the tedious de-briefing and post action reports began. First their TPF Sergeant wanted to know if they were alright. Then Detectives showed up wanting to know who shot who, where were Red and Sean during the gun battle. A department shooting team arrived and taped off the entire area, locating and marking all the shell casings. Then they took Red and Sean's weapons for lab analysis. Next the "Brass" showed up. The four-star Chief of Patrol and a Deputy Commissioner had spoken to the Detectives, then came over to Red and Sean to shake their hands.

"Well done men, you certainly put the spotlight on the TPF" said the Deputy Commissioner.

"Good job, this was one hell of a stop, congratulations" said the Chief of Patrol.

Both men said thank you as the two high officials left the scene. Next to arrive was the Forensics Team followed by the black morgue wagon. The Medical Examiner was with the detectives for no more than ten minutes when six body bags were loaded into the wagon. Then a series of unmarked cars arrived. Red and Sean watched as the Mayor and Police Commissioner exited and began speaking to a Deputy Chief. The press was arriving and setting up their cameras and microphones. The Mayor came over.

"Officers Blackman and Feeney, you are to be commended for a job well done."

They both nodded.

Then the Police Commissioner,

"Boys the press is going to make you two bigger than a Macy Balloon, just be humble."

Then they both walked away back to their black unmarked vehicle and were gone. A Lieutenant of Public Affairs came over and said,

"You both are advised not to speak to the media at this time, there will another time for that.

Arrangements have been made to transport you both to your homes. We will be in touch with you the next day. Am I clear on this, gentlemen?"

"Crystal sir."

As he left Red looked at Sean and said,

"Feeney me boy, good things are about to happen to us."

"Rabbi Blackman from your mouth to God's ear."

They both laughed and walked toward the patrol cars.

CHAPTER SIXTEEN

The Next Day – Police Headquarters
1961

Headline: The New York Daily News
BIG BANK SHOOTOUT IN THE BRONX

Headline: The New York Daily Mirror
THE BRONX MASSACRE

Headline: The New York Post
COPS WIN BRONX SHOOTOUT

Headline: The New York Times
A BRONX TRAGEDY

Every television station covered the bank robbery and shootout and wanted an exclusive interview with the two hero cops, but the NYPD Press Office kept everyone away. Red and Sean were brought to Police Headquarters. In a conference room they were briefed on the follow up of the robbery. A Detective Lieutenant by the name of Martino started.

"We have identified the dead bank employees as

Martin Dyer, age 58, Bank Guard

Cynthia Stoddard, age 25, Teller

Gloria Holden, age 31, Teller

Branch Manager Roger White remains in critical condition at Montefiore Hospital.

The dead perpetrators were identified as,

L.D. Benton, 32, San Antonio, Texas

Terrence Kelly, 29, Baltimore, Maryland

Martin London, 38, Huntington, Kentucky.

The captured suspect was,

Harold Hilliard, 42, Roanoke Virginia

The car that was the getaway car was stolen in Richmond, Virginia two weeks prior to this robbery.

This group was known as the Hilliard gang and were wanted nationwide in eight bank robberies in eight different states. Harold Hilliard will be turned over to Federal authorities and prosecuted in Federal court. Ballistic testing was conducted and compared to bullets removed during the autopsies and revealed Hilliard's weapon killed the three-bank employee and shot Manager White. Officer's Feeney weapon killed both Benton and Kelly, while bullets from Officer's Blackman weapon killed driver Martin London. The amount of money recovered was one million eight hundred and eighty-seven thousand dollars. The interdiction of Officers Blackman and Feeney stopped a gang that had been terrorizing the country."

Martino finished and stepped away from the podium. Next a man in a three-piece suit came up.

"Hello, my name is Edward Markham, I am an Associate Director of the FBI, Washington, D.C. I head up the National Bank Robbery Task Force. We have been chasing this crew for the past four years. Officers Blackman and Feeney, you have taken off the streets a very dangerous group of career criminals. Harold Hilliard will be charged with ten counts of murder in the First Degree, nine counts of Bank Robbery, six counts of violent assault and attempted murder. Once again, thank you."

The Mayor and Police Commissioner took centerstage. Red and Sean were called up to the podium.

Commissioner spoke first,

"Officers Blackman and Feeney, it is not often we have seen such bravery under fire. It is my honor to present each of you with the NYPD Combat Cross for your heroism and dedication to duty that reflect the highest standards of the Department."

With the medal draped by a blue green ribbon it was placed around their necks by the commissioner.

Now the Mayor spoke,

"You two officers performed brilliantly in a very quick and dangerous situation. Both of you displayed initiative and extreme bravery. To just award a medal for this action is not enough. It is within my power to make appointments in all city departments. Today you are both promoted to Detective Grade

Three. Here are your Gold Shields. The people of the City of New York thank you for your bravery and dedication."

Red and Sean each received a leather wallet containing their Gold Shields. They hugged each other, then shook hands with those in the room. With the ceremony ending soon they were all alone in the room. They had achieved their shared goal, and now there was one more step to conquer, and that was going to be answered by the man who now entered the room. They both stood up for they recognized him as their new boss. Chief of Detectives Ronald Stowall said,

"Sit down guys this will not take long. Welcome to the Detective Bureau. Blackman you report Friday to the 4th Detective Squad in Manhattan, and Feeney you're in the 47th Squad in the Bronx. Welcome aboard and good luck."

Sean,

"No Sir, that is not good enough. Red and I are a team and either we work together or put us back in the TPF where we can continue to work as partners."

"Well Detective Feeney that is not going to happen. I'm the boss and you go where I send you, do you agree Detective Blackman?"

"I believe you will get a better bang for your dollar if we stay together. Look, we have seen and worked in the sewers of this department, and we're talking the precincts. That was not why we became cops. It would be a very wise and politically astute move if you to have the most recent winners of the Combat

Cross remain as a team. Why Chief Stowall, you would be lauded. Keep us together and we guarantee you will see results. You know the places where we can do the most good, send us there."

Stowall had underestimated these two, but most of all he knew the politics of the department. There was an unwritten rule, never screw with bona fide hero cops for they can do a lot of personal damage if you piss them off.

"Ok you two pirates, report to the 102nd Squad in Queens, and you better not fuck up."

He turned and left the room.

Sean smiling,

"We did it Red."

"Right on partner, that's the only language he understood."

CHAPTER SEVENTEEN

102nd Detective Squad, Queens
1961

The 102nd Precinct was a dirty non-descript structure located off a busy avenue. The building needed a paint job, the front desk was old wood that needed a polishing and smelled of smoke and stale food.

They showed their shield to the Desk Sergeant and said,

"Blackman and Feeney reporting in"

"Go upstairs and turn right, your expected."

The staircase was wide and dirty. At the top they found a door with a glass panel that could have used a replacement. On the glass in gold letters was written "102n Squa". The letters d and q were missing.

Both of them thought Stowall knew where he was sending them, he must be laughing now. Inside was a large room with desks, chairs, typewriters, telephones a prisoner cage and several private offices on the side. It smelled of smoke, human perspiration, and stale food. The one positive point was that it was busy. There were two prisoners in handcuffs in the cage, six detectives were at their desks either typing, or taking statements from civilians. They saw a door marked "Sergeant", knocked and heard a voice to enter. Behind the desk his eyes were focused on a report. He looked up and said,

"Wyatt Earp and Wild Bill Hickok sit down, welcome to the 102nd Squad. Your reputations precede you.

I'm Sgt. Byron Crandall, I'm second in command to Lt. Casey. This is a busy shop and we have good people working here. You two will learn from them and you have a three-month probation period to show command if you are worth to take on your own cases. A couple of rules. Never lie or coverup, no freelancing, stay within the command structure and learn from your mistakes. I'll take you into the Lt. he'll assign you to a veteran detective. Oh, by the way we call the Lieutenant, "Lou", a department tradition.

Which of you is Blackman?"

"I am".

"Since I cannot tell you both apart, we will call you Red. Is that ok?

"No problems Sergeant"

Crandall got up and took them the Lieutenant's office. He knocked and they heard enter. The nameplate said Lt. Douglas Casey. Behind the desk was a big stern looking man about 45 years old. He had a bottle of milk of magnesia on his desk.

'Sit down Byron. You two remain standing.

"So, you're the wonder kids they sent me. Which one of you is Feeney?

Sean raised his hand.

"I see by your file your one hell of shot, broke the Academy record."

"Yes."

"Let me inspect your weapon"

Sean withdrew the revolver, opened the chamber, removed the six bullets and handed the empty gun to the Lieutenant.

"Why are you carrying a .357 Magnum revolver, .38 Special is department issue?"

"Sir, that is what I was issued for TPF, nobody ever asked for it back. We both have .357's"

Casey looked at Crandall and shrugged.

"Well we always could use a little more firepower. Until they find their mistake keep it on your hip.

He looked at Blackman.

And you must be the Honor Cadet. What have you learned so far in your brief police career?"

"I know there is wide disparity between Academy teachings and the street. I know there are cops out there who are corrupt and would not lift a hand to help you. I know that this department reacts to the political climate and sometimes forgetting the basics of their mission goal to protect the public. And I know that what took Sean and I stand here right now was a direct result of our own merits."

Casey again looked at Crandall but this time he smiled.

"You will be assigned a veteran detective for a three-month period. Your work will be evaluated after that period. If you do not cut the mustard, you will be re-assigned to someplace but not to a squad. So, listen and follow orders, Welcome Detectives to the 102nd, Sgt. Crandall will now assign your professors for the next three months. Good luck."

They left the Lieutenant's office. Crandall told Sean to take a seat. He had Red follow him over to a desk.

"Red, this is Detective First Grade Joe Williams. Joe this is Detective Third Grade Morris Blackman, call him Red."

Williams was a tall lanky fellow with longish brown hair. He told Red to sit while he finished the papers on his desk. For about fifteen minutes Red just sat and watched when Williams raised his head and said,

"Look I'm sorry. I'm not trying to ignore you, but this is an important case. I need all this for a court appearance two days from now."

"That's alright I'm not offended. Is there any way I can help?"

Williams smiled and said.

"Sure, you can put these in date order, thanks."

Red took a pile of papers and found an empty desk. He started compiling and separating. As he worked, he could not help but notice the case was against a Marvin Schotski for running a running an illegal lottery. As he continued to scan each page it became clearer that the term illegal lottery was a legal term for running numbers on the street. Schotski was first investigated about a year ago. It started with a player reporting Schotski was using strong arm tactics in the neighborhoods. Numerous beatings and destruction of property had been reported but never tied to this individual. Schotski was not your local small numbers guy. He was county wide with drops throughout the borough. Surveillance by Williams had uncovered an operation at 672-88th Street near Rockway Boulevard. This building housed Schotski's main operation. On a daily basis over 145 people were observed entering and leaving the building carrying paper shopping bags. There was a photograph of Schotski as well as videotape of him arriving in a Mercedes Benz accompanied by a driver and two bodyguards. He is seen leaving with a black suitcase. The investigation continues with a raid on the premises during an afternoon in April. As Red continues reading his eyes widen when he reads that cash amounting to $8.6 million was found and confiscated as evidence. Taken into custody were Schotski and fourteen of his employees. At interview Schotski would not talk and asked for his attorney. He was booked and made the $2 million bail bond. Red was now down to the last pages. He saw a note that copied the NYPD Organized Crime Unit. It stated Schotski was a known associate of the Bonnano Crime Family since 1958. The last page was the court ordered appearance of Detective Joseph Williams for the trial start in two days.

"Here they are in date order."

He handed the pile to Williams.

"Thanks, this helps a lot. You look like you have some questions."

"I know this a big case. What were the strong-arm tactics?

"Schotski needed legitimate locations for his runners to take the numbers, so he muscled some storeowners, and one of them did not cooperate. This guy was a registered pharmacist and owned his own pharmacy. He did not want his name, nor his business associated with gambling. Schotki's driver and bodyguard put him in the hospital. The pharmacists wife came forward and put us onto him. She agreed to meet with Schotski and cooperate with him. He could use the premises, and she would operate the pharmacy. We brought in a registered pharmacist as a replacement for her husband and had a young undercover cop inside working as sales help. We had sound and video wire inside and outside the store.

We got enough on Schotski to put his operation down for a long time."

Red asks,

"With all the time you put into this, how did you get your daily work done?"

"Whenever you have a case that involves one of the Five Families, the resources you have at your disposal are unlimited. I had a once a week meeting downtown with the Organized Task Force and went over the surveillance material they had gathered. I decided to do the raid on April Fool's Day, just to provide some humor. All during this period I was able to maintain being lead investigator and was able to do my regular squad duties. The Queens DA is very confident Schotski will be vacationing upstate for a least fifteen years."

"Congratulations Detective."

"Thanks, but call me Joe, and you?"

"Call me Red."

"Hey you like Chinese, my treat."

"Hell yeah, that's Jewish soul food."

"If your kosher, I know a kosher Chinese place."

"No, I am not kosher, and I like the real McCoy."

"I like you already Red."

While Williams and Red were talking, Sean was working with Detective First Grade Gus Antaknockis.

Antaknockis a 2nd generation Greek American, was just under 6 feet tall, but was a wide 240 lbs. His neck must have measured twenty inches, yet you could see he was light on his feet.

"So, if I'm going to train you for three months tell me where you come from?"

"Woodhaven"

"I'm from Brooklyn, Sean. On the job 14 years with the last seven spent here. This is a good squad, the Lou and Sarge are tough but fair. They want the brass away from here, and the way you do that is closed cases."

"How is your record?"

"I'm at an 89% closure rate.

"That is pretty good. What are the majority of cases around here?"

"Mostly burglaries, street assaults, trafficking in stolen goods and even homicides. Here's a case I got yesterday. You read the preliminary report and tell me what you think."

Sean took the file and started reading.

>Investigation: Home Break In
>Case number: 8655672349
>Investigators: G. Antaknockis W. Earley
>Scene of report: 345 27th Road, Queens, N Y
>Time Reported: 1750 hrs. of 3/28/1961
>Initial responders: Ptlmn. Barros and Ivens
>Investigator Arrival time: 1823 hours
>Victim(s): Darryl Lattimore, homeowner
>Point of entry: Front door
>Items Missing: RCA Color Television set
>Serial No.: None given
>Estimated Value: $600.00
>Insured: Yes

INITIAL INVESTIGATION

Found no forcible entry on front door. No forcible entry on rear door. TV set was a console model and would be impossible to get through windows. Victim is unmarried and lives alone. Victim found the TV missing when he entered premises. He stated he was coming home from work. Notable items observed were a Sterling Silver tea service, a men's diamond ring in the bedroom and three paintings victim claimed were bought for $3500.00.

SECONDARY INVESTIGATION

Canvassed the neighborhood and found no reported burglaries. Owner of property across the street did not see anyone in the immediate area but did state victim had a live-in female. Description: W F Black hair, very attractive and drives a White Chrysler convertible.

Put out notices to Pawn Network NYC

Investigator departure time: 1910 hours.

Sean finished reading and looked at Gus.

"First no forcible entry. Somebody had a key. Victim and his girlfriend may have had a quarrel, she takes it out on him by grabbing the TV set. The perp does not take anything else, maybe the TV set belonged to the girlfriend. I can only guess that she needed help to get it into her car back seat."

"Very good. You picked up some good points. Well we found the girlfriend and it was her TV.

They had broken up about a week before the call. Even the girlfriend called it. She said he would file a

a $600.00 insurance claim. He did, and we charged him with Insurance fraud. He pleaded guilty

paid a $1000.00 dollar fine in lieu of jail time. Case closed."

"You get a lot of these type of cases?"

"At least two a month. They all have to be investigated, and you have to put in your time. So, if we get a homicide or a big heist, we will work round the clock until we capture the perp. In regard to the case you just read, the case breaker was the neighbor across the street for his info broke it open. The rule that comes down from the Lou and Sgt. is never take anything for granted, go the extra mile and check everything. Ok, are you ready to tour our beautiful neighborhood?"

"Sure, let's go."

CHAPTER EIGHTEEN

The Ride
1961

The tour of the precinct was nothing extraordinary. Lacking the glimmer and sense of urgency that a Manhattan exudes, Queens was dull, rundown and somehow waiting for the word "go" to be said. Gus drove along Rockaway Boulevard pointing out the best place for breakfast, the best Chinese food, the best Greek diner, the best Pizza place, and even the best dirty water hot dog vendor. He stopped and doubled parked, got out and ran into a shop called, Athena's Coffee and Pastry. He came back with 2 cups of coffee and a bag of pastries.

"Here, try these tell me how you like them."

Sean grabbed a pastry that looked like a Cheese Danish, and bit into it, followed by a gulp of coffee. It tasted like cheesecake and it was wonderful, and the coffee was the best he ever had.

"Wow Gus, everything is delicious. What's the pastry called?"

"Milopita, and my cousin Athena thanks you."

"You got a lot a family in Queens?"

"I got family all over New York, if I walk into a Greek diner in Staten Island, they're probably relatives."

Gus started up and began pointing out places of interest. At the corner of Rockaway and Inwood he pointed out a barbershop.

"Jackie the Barber was a fence during the fifties. I got him on possession of stolen goods. He did not want to do time, so he cooperated. We ended up busting a larger group that grabbed high end merch out of Idlewild Airport. Jackie got out of the business and went to barber school. I sometimes get a haircut there just to hear the gossip on the street."

At 145th Street he pointed to a place called San Juan Car Painting.

"That is owned by a friend of mine, Juan Mercado. They do not paint cars; they chop them up. Want to know anything about cars Juan is the guy."

"If he is chopping up stolen cars, why don't you arrest him?"

"Good question kid. Let me explain something that was taught to me by the Lou. Yes, by our oath we are obligated to arrest all involved in crime. However, each and everything we find that is in violation of the law has a higher entity above it. Sure, Juan can be arrested and shutdown, but will that stop another Chop Shop from opening down the street, no. What we concentrate on is who is Juan answering to, who is calling the bigger shots, those are the guys we want for that is where the bigger money is located. Juan may be sending the parts to a warehouse on the waterfront. That is owned by a group of criminals who make money putting those parts on boats to South America. In order for them to operate they pay for the right to do their work in an area belonging to a higher and more sophisticated criminal network. This last group are the ones we're going after. You get a lead on them, you work it till you got them between the rock and the hard place, then they are yours and you the hunter can come home from the hill. Do you understand?"

"I understand, but what about a Homicide?"

"Homicide cases are a race between you and the clock. If you do not even get a faint sniff of the perp within the first 48 hours, you will fail to close it. Figure a homicide is like the marathon in the Olympics, you will not win if you sprint the whole 26 miles, but you'll have a chance if you pace yourself and then strike at the proper time."

At the corner of 140th and Rockaway Gus pointed to a gas station.

"That's were Jimmy Fleherty got it."

"Who was he?"

A Detective on the squad. In 1959 pulled in there on his way home to fill up. He is sitting in his car with the gas hose pumping away. A van pulls in and two masked assholes jump out and head into the garage.

They were there to take the money. They shoot the owner; Jimmy hears the shots and gets out of his car. The van driver cuts him into half with a shotgun, he never saw it. Left a wife and three kids. Sgt. Crandall and Fleherty were partners. The squad went full out on this, we worked 72 hours, slept in the interview room and we got them. All three got the chair, but they're still alive awaiting appeals."

Sean was quiet realizing he had so much to learn about this job. Just then Gus pulled over and parked at the curb.

"Sean, in the backseat are a bunch of caps, pull out the Yankee cap and place it in the rear window. I just got a hand signal from one of my street informers. We'll meet him in the alley a block up."

"What's with the ballcaps?"

"That's Detective SOP, every day the cap changes. You get out of the car it tells the patrol guys your working, go away, no tickets."

As they start walking Sean asks,

"So what cap is for what day?"

"Today Is Monday -Yankee day

Tuesday -Rangers Day

Wednesday – Knicks

Thursday – Giants

Friday – Mets

Saturday – Jets

Sunday- St, Johns"

They reached the alley and waited behind a laundromat. A door opened and a male black wearing a Boston Celtic t shirt and jeans came out.

Gus says,

"Hey Spider, what's up? This is my partner, Sean."

Spider nodded towards Sean, then spoke.

"I heard that Waldo Cammerata is out of prison, and he is forming a crew."

"How good was the source?"

"Real good, he knew Waldo from the joint."

"Waldo's back, the boys in the squad will love to hear that. Listen Spider, get me more info on the job he's planning, and I'll make it worth your while."

Gus pulled out his wallet and handed Spider two twenty-dollar bills. Spider takes the money and heads up the alley.

Sean asks,

"What was that all about and why are you handing out your own cash?"

"Sean, that guy Spider is one of my sources I got on the street. About five years ago, I busted him for heroin possession, he was scared to death about going to jail for three years, so I turned him. We have a gentleman's agreement, I don't bust him for drugs, he lets me know when big things are going down. Waldo Cammerata is big news because he is a strong-arm robbery expert. If he is getting a crew together, the crime stats will go up. You will see high dollar robberies and a lot of injured people. He and I go back to the fifties. I sent him up for assault with a deadly weapon. He got six years and was out in two. Waldo is a dangerous tornado and needs to be watched and taken down. As far as my personal money goes it is used for that information and the Department is not going to have a bag of money available. Everyone on the squad does it because these street people see and hear everything and have very little. If we need to do our jobs and be successful, we need these people and their information. Spider got $40 bucks, but he knows there is more if he tells me Waldo's plan."

"So how much do you spend on these informants?"

"Runs me about $500 a year to be the community chest."

"Is it worth it?"

"It is when you have an 89% closure rate. It's the cost of doing business so you can be the cop they trained you to be."

CHAPTER NINETEEN

Homicide Case
1961

The phone rang in the Squad Room, Joe picked it up. He listened and wrote down an address. Looking at Red he said,

"We got a homicide on Linden Boulevard, let's move."

It took them about ten minutes to arrive at 6521 Linden Boulevard. The patrol cops that first responded escorted them up to a third-floor apartment. Williams asked one of the uniforms,

"How did you find the body?"

"We responded to shots fired, the neighbors told us it was upstairs. Found the door open, went inside maybe six feet, saw the body in the bedroom. My partner checked to see if he was alive. No breathing, lots of blood loss, called it in to the Sergeant.

"Where's your Sergeant?"

"In the kitchen waiting for you."

They entered the apartment, saw the Sergeant sitting at the kitchen counter. He introduced himself to the Detectives as Sgt. Meredith. Williams spoke first,

"Sergeant we need a perimeter set up. Have one your men start canvassing the apartments on this floor. I am going to need a scene log in officer to stand outside and check everyone in and out, recording the time. If you can get a hold of the building superintendent, let me know if they have cameras installed that would be appreciated."

Meredith responded.

"You got it."

Joe saw the patrol officer who would do the scene check in and said,

"Patrolman, what is your name and your partner's name?

"I'm Patrolman Edward Tobias and my partner is Lawrence Russo."

"Good, in your sign in log, write down the time you and your partner entered this apartment. The time your Sergeant entered. My name is Williams and this is my partner Blackman, put us in as entering about 2 minutes ago."

"Yes Sir."

"Officer Tobias, when we are finished here you and your partner will be the last to leave. Upon returning to the Precinct you make sure that log is sent immediately to my attention; Detective Williams – 102nd Squad. Got that?"

"Yes Sir."

"Thank you, Officer Tobias."

"Red we never touch or move the body until the Medical Examiner shows up. Meanwhile check for evidence. Do not touch it or move it but note the location. When the photographer shows up show him all the things you found. The we wait for Forensics to bag it."

"I understand."

Red moved outward from the body. In an ashtray he found cigarette butts. Looking closer he noticed one was a Newport the other a Pall Mall. The Newport had lipstick on it. In the bathroom he found two towels hanging, one was moist the other dry. The sink showed some strands of long blond hair. The medicine cabinet had several prescription bottles labeled from a pharmacy in Cos Cob, Connecticut for one Gerard Conolly. In the kitchen he saw dishes in the sink and two wine glasses. One of the wine glasses had lipstick on it. Opening the refrigerator, he found a wrapped beef roast, some of which was carved. In the garbage can under the sink was an empty bottle of Rothschild Maison 1931 vintage. He then heard Williams call him from the bedroom. As he entered, he saw a man with a jacket that said ME Williams moving the body. Williams looked up and said,

"Red this is Doctor Ted Stiles from the ME Office, Bob this Detective Morris Blackman."

"Hello Detective. I take it this is your Homicide Investigation, well just watch and see what I do."

Williams comments,

"Wait a minute Doc, Bobby Timko wants to take some photographs."

They waited and watched as the photographer took some twenty shots of the body from various angles, he nodded to the Doc he was finished. The ME turned the body over and said,

"One shot through the heart, no exit wound. Bullet still inside the body. No trauma to the head or neck.

Fingernails appear to be manicured. "

He reached into his bag and pulled out a magnifying glass and examined the victims right hand.

"There appears to be some residue under his right middle fingernail, I will scrape and bag."

He then took a needle like instrument and inserted it in the victim's belly area and waited a few minutes.

Removing it he said,

"Liver temperature is 72 degrees, he has been dead for three hours.

He examined the victims groin area and noticed a light stain on white briefs. Taking out a flashlight he turned it on an it emitted a blue light causing the faint stain to be highly illuminated.

"Victim had an ejaculation before he died."

He examined the victim's legs and feet and found nothing noteworthy.

"Ok Joe that is it for me, the autopsy should tell us a lot more. You can go through his pants pockets and when you finish call in my guys, and they will bag him. Nice meeting you Detective Blackman hope you learned something."

"Yes, I did Dr. Stiles, thank you."

Joe had removed the victim's wallet, a gold watch from his wrist, and a ticket from a parking garage.

In the wallet was some $3000 in cash, several credit cards, a Connecticut Driver's License for one Gerard Conolly, 135 Runyon Lane, Cos Cob, CT. His age was listed at 54. The watch was a solid gold Rolex and band. There was a gold pinky ring on his left hand that contained what looked like a diamond.

"Red, please bag all of this. We take this back with us and turn it in as evidence. Look at this parking claim check, what do you see?

Red took the claim check and saw that it was for a garage about a block away. The time stamp was for yesterday at 1130 PM.

"It looks like his car may be there."

"Go ahead and check it out, leave me your evidence notes and I will work with the photographer."

Red went up to Officer Tobias and said,

"Sign me out now, I'm going to Metro Parking at 178th Street, please put that down."

"Yes Sir.'

He got to the parking garage in five minutes. Identified himself as a Police Officer and instructed the attendant to bring the key and show him where the car was located. On the third level he found a 1961 Blue Mercedes 220SE. He noted the Connecticut plate GC 1776. Opening the door, he looked in touching nothing. Opening the trunk, he found nothing. He relocked the car. With the car identified as the same belonging to the claim, he made a phone call from the garage office.

"NYPD non-emergency line, how can I direct your call?"

"This is Detective Blackman, 102nd Squad, require a tow truck respond for vehicle pickup at Metro Parking number 36 178th Street, Queens. Active Homicide case."

"Detective the tow is enroute will arrive 20 minutes."

"Thank you."

He waited for twenty-two minutes when the tow arrived. Red went back to the third level with driver and watched him hook up and made sure he touched nothing. Red got a receipt from the driver and the time noted. With the Mercedes in tow, the driver dropped Red off at the crime scene, then left for the NYPD Crime Lab.

Red checked back in with Officer Tobias and saw Joe talking to a man in the kitchen. He waited for Joe to finish, and Joe told the man thank you and he left.

Red told Joe about the car and that is was on the way to the lab.

"Good job, that guy was the super of the building, Stanley Belcik. Conolly has been here for four years, good tenant and always paid in cash and on time. I ask him if Conolly lived alone or with someone else? He said mostly alone, but he saw some beautiful women with him at times. Asked if he saw anyone last night, and he said he saw no one."

The last of the Forensic crew were finishing up. They had bagged and tagged and swiped for fingerprints.

"Well we're about finished here, let's check out"

Red asks,

"Are we going back to the Squad?

"No my student, we are going to Cos Cob to notify the next of kin."

"Don't we usually call the local Police to make the notice?"

"Yes, we could but I want to see the reaction. Maybe they did it. Call ahead to the Cos Cob PD and have them meet us at Conolly's home."

The trip from Queens took about 50 minutes with red lights and siren. Arriving at the Conolly address they were met by a uniformed Cos Cob officer. Explaining the situation, they followed the patrol car down the driveway. The grounds were beautiful, and the house was a red brick mansion. The patrolman rang the bell, and the door was opened by a butler. The officer requested to see Mrs. Conolly and were shown inside. The house reeked of wealth. In a few minutes an elegantly dressed women in her late forties appeared. Red noted she was a brunette.

"I'm Marilyn Conolly, is there a problem?

"Mrs. Conolly, I am Detective Williams, and this is Detective Blackman of the New York Police Department. I regret to inform you that your husband Gerard Conolly was found dead this afternoon. our condolences."

She immediately cringed, found a chair sat down and started crying. A maid arrived and started to console her. They stood there for about five minutes, then she wiped her eyes and asked,

"How did Gerard die?"

"He was shot once."

"Was he in his office?"

"No Ma 'me, he was found in his Queens apartment."

"What apartment in Queens? He never had an apartment in Queens. If he needed to stay in the city, it was always at the Pierre."

"Your husband rented an apartment in Queens for the last four years."

She looked perturbed and hurt.

"Mrs. Conolly, do you know if your husband had any enemies?"

"No, he never mentioned anyone."

"What was your husband's line of work?"

"He was president of Conolly Investments, 145 Wall Street."

"Are there any family members we can talk to?"

"Our oldest is married and living in the United Kingdom, she works for the Bank of England, and our other child is on a scientific survey of Chile, he is a full professor at the University of Michigan. They only come home at Christmas."

"I am sorry for your loss, but we require the next of kin to identify his body at the Queens County Medical Examiner's Office so the body can be released for burial. Detective Blackman will provide you with the address, here is my card if you remember anything pertinent to this investigation. Once again our condolences."

Williams and the Cos Cob officer left, while Red gave her the information. Back in the car Red asked,

"Get anything out of this?"

"A lot, she had no idea of what her husband was doing, if she did, they would have been divorced long ago. He played her by keeping her in constant luxury. No, old Gerard was a fox. I got this idea that this case revolves around big money, but let's let the evidence do the talking. The game is on my young and eager student, we will have a lot to do before this is over."

CHAPTER TWENTY

New York State Supreme Court-Country of Queens
State vs. Marvin Schotski
1961

Red followed Joe into the courtroom. They were lucky Joe's appearance was in the afternoon, at least they got some sleep. Joe met with Assistant District Attorney Lena Oliver and her staff.

"Detective Williams we are going to lead off with your testimony. Please keep it simple and straight.

His lawyers of course are going to poke holes, so be prepared."

Williams stated,

"I'm ready."

Joe and Red took seats behind the prosecutor's table and the trial began as Judge Smithson took his seat. To the right of the prosecutor sat in all his grandeur Marvin Schotski. Dressed in a dark gray suit with a purple tie, he smiled as if he didn't have a care in the world. The jury had been picked the previous week were brought in and seated. Lena Oliver presented the case for the State. She was followed by Schotski's attorney, Paul Osterman, stating his plan for the defense. The first witness called was Detective Joe Williams. Joe stood and took the oath then sat down in the box. Red was amazed how calm he appeared. All his paperwork and notes were left with Red for he had committed everything to memory. He had told Red that if a defense attorney saw you referring to notes, they would try and get it admitted "Detective Williams what is your rank and where do you work?"

"I am a Detective First Grade and work out of the 102nd Squad."

"How many years have you been a detective in the NYPD?"

"Fourteen years a Detective, seventeen with the Department".

"When did you start this investigation?"

"One year ago, this past Monday."

"On what information was Mr. Marvin Schotski brought to your attention?"

"I received a tip from a confidential informant that the defendant was using strong arms tactics in expanding his business operation."

"What kind of business was the defendant operating?"

"An illegal lottery, better known as the numbers racket. It operated at several county locations."

"Did you perform surveillance of these operations?"

"Yes. We followed the money pickups to a central collection office located at 692 88th Street. We observed and recorded on a daily basis one hundred and forty persons entering this location."

"These one hundred and forty persons, was there anything distinct about their arrivals at the 88th Street location?"

"Each person was observed filling paper shopping bags with cash from other surveilled locations, leaving those locations and observed arriving and entering the defendant's 88th Street locale carrying the same bag. All entered and exited the building."

"Upon leaving the 88th Street locale was anything noticeable?"

"Yes, upon leaving they no longer carried the paper shopping bags."

"Did your investigation uncover charges of "strong arm" tactics?"

"Yes. An owner of a pharmacy was approached by associates of the defendant. They needed to use his store as a number's drop. The owner refused, he was assaulted very badly, and was in the hospital for five months."

"My last question Detective. Was the defendant Marvin Schotski involved in this assault?"

"Yes. We have a tape recording from the wife of the pharmacist indicating that the defendant by name would do the same to her if she did not co-operate."

"Thank you, Detective Williams."

Defense Attorney Osterman was next.

"Detective Williams, my client is a small businessman with limited means. It amazes me that he is being charged for this. We all know numbers are run out the corner candy store and are usually located in small quiet neighborhoods. My Lord, the prosecution has made this out to be a vast criminal enterprise."

Before Osterman could continue, Joe interrupted him knowing full well he was out of order.

"Well it is Mr. Osterman."

"Your Honor I object, the witness is offering a personal opinion."

"Objection sustained; the witness will refrain from offering opinions. Members of the jury you are to dismiss the witness's response."

Red smiled, Joe was a cagey fox he wanted the jury to hear that. Now their interest was piqued.

Attorney Osterman continued.

"Detective Williams could these paper shopping bags be lunch bags that these one and forty persons were carrying?"

No, they were filled with cash. When they entered the 88th Street locale, they walked in and then they walked out. If they ate their lunch in that span of time that would be an incredible feat."

"I object your Honor; the witness is offering an opinion again."

Just then the ADA stood up.

"Your Honor he is badgering the witness."

"Objection overruled. The witness was not stating an opinion, it sounded like a fact to me. Proceed Mr. Osterman."

"On April 1, 1961 Detective Williams did you have a search warrant the day 692 88th Street was raided?"

"Yes, duly signed by Judge Horace Meader, Queens County Supreme Court."

"During that raid did you find the defendant on the premises?"

"No, we did not."

"Your Honor I am finished with this witness."

ADA Oliver spoke.

"Your Honor the State would like to re-examine Detective Williams."

Judge replies,

"You may re-examine."

Red took note of Joe looking at the ADA. He gave her a brief smile.

"Detective Williams on March 31, 1961 was there a surveillance of 692 88th Street?"

"Yes."

"What was observed?"

"At 5PM on that date we observed, and video recorded a black Mercedes Benz drive up to the location.

Two bodyguards got out, one opened the passenger door and the defendant Marvin Schotski got out. He was not carrying anything at this time. He entered the building in the company of his two bodyguards. Approximately fifteen minutes later another Mercedes pulled up. One bodyguard opened the passenger door and a single male got out and entered the same premises that the defendant has recently entered.

The observed person did not carry anything into the building. There was a time span of some twenty minutes when both the defendant and this single male appeared outside the premises both carrying black briefcases. They shook hands and got into their respective vehicles and left in different directions. Both vehicles were followed. Defendant Schotski proceeded to his residence in Queens, while the unidentified male was followed to a private residence in Manhattan."

"Your Honor I would like to re-call this witness. I request that I call for the state another witness vital to this case.?"

"You may call your witness, Ms. Oliver."

"The State calls Special Agent William Baxter of the FBI."

Red watched as a well-dressed middle age male made his way to the witness box and took the oath.

"Please state your name and position?"

"William Baxter, Special Agent FBI Eastern District of New York, US Department of Justice."

"Agent Baxter do you head up a special task force?"

"Yes, I am the head of the Organized Crime Task Force for the Eastern District."

"How do you know Detective Joseph Williams?"

"Detective Williams brought us this information regarding their surveillance of 692 88th Street on March 31, 1961. We were able to determine a connection with our own investigation. Detective Williams was seconded to our task force."

"Can you identify the male who met with defendant at the 88th Street locale, and left with him from that locale?"

"Yes, his name is Carmine Frischetti."

"And who does Mr. Frischetti represent?"

"He is the number two underboss in the Genovese Crime Family."

Red could see Marvin Schotski straighten up in his chair as if he was electrocuted. There was an immediate conference between him and his attorney. The conversation became animated, and it became louder.

This drew the attention of ADA Oliver who turned to the judge and said,

"Your Honor, I am finished with this witness, subject to recall."

The judge looked at the defendant's attorney, who was still heavily involved with his client.

"Mr. Osterman do you wish to cross-examine this witness?"

Osterman did not immediately reply and had to be asked again by the bench. The flustered attorney stood up and replied."

"No, your Honor."

ADA Oliver then recalled Williams

"Detective can you tell the jury what you found and confiscated on the April 1, 1961 raid of 692 88th Street for which you had a duly signed search warrant?"

"We found paper shopping bags full of cash and the numbers to be played."

"How much cash did you confiscate from that premises?"

"We confiscated $8.6 million dollar in cash."

In the jury box the jurors sat up and took note. At the defense table the attorney and defendant were whispering so close they looked like Siamese twins.

"Now that $8.6 million constituted how many days take?"

"Ms. Oliver that was one day's take. Mr. Schotski's business took that in on an average daily basis."

The jury shook their heads and stared at the defendant. That was all Marvin Schotski could take. He buried his face in his hands and laid his head on the table. Attorney Osterman rose up and said.

"Your Honor, my client wishes to change his plea to guilty and forego this trial."

It was over. Joe congratulated the prosecutor and thanked Agent Baxter. Red came over and asked.

"Why did he plead guilty? He'll be going away for some long time."

"Marvin had a "come to Jesus" moment do the time or incur the wrath of the Genovese Family. He made the right decision. If he's a good boy, he'll be out in six. Let's get us a drink, then get back to solving that Homicide."

CHAPTER TWENTY-ONE

NY State Offices, Queens Boulevard
1961

Gus and Sean had a meeting with Waldo Cammerata's parole officer. They entered the Office of

State Parole and asked to see Fred Tunison. Tunison came out and greeted them. He was about 5 feet 9 inches and must have weighed in the 260 area. He wore glasses and had about four pens in his shirt pocket. One would say this guy looks overworked and probably counting the days to his retirement. Sean thought to himself what a crappy job trying to keep on top of a bunch criminals who would repeat their crimes.

Gus lead off the conversation.

"Thanks for meeting with us Mr. Tunison. What can you tell us about Waldo Cammarata?"

"Well he reported in on time for the last three Thursdays. Said he had a job at an autobody shop, which I still have to check on. So far, no problems, but I'm sure something will come up, he's a career criminal with things to do."

"We got a tip he may be raising a crew for a job. So, we would like to see where he says he is working."

Tunison checked the folder he was holding.

"Casino Auto Body 687 South Conduit Avenue."

"Thank you, Sir, we'll save you a trip and let you know if he is there."

Tunison replied,

"That certainly would save me a trip and time, thank you."

Sean,

"If he is not working and we tell you. How long will it be before he is sent back for his parole violation?

Tunison. Answered,

"From the time I file the paperwork to the actual apprehension could take some three months. That is why the system is broken."

"Thank you for your time."

On the ride down to the body shop Sean asked,

"Gus, what if Cammarata is not there?"

"Then it is just one more checkoff that he is planning to do a job. We will call Tunison and nothing will happen because he's over his head with work. Instead, we put out a call for his location, information only. Hit our street people, they will tell us what is on the 'Street Telegraph'. Sean, this guy sat for a few years in a small cell just thinking and thinking about his next score. While on the inside he got some of the best intelligence on what to knock over. We will need to know who was his cellmate? Who did he hang with in prison? We have to learn who he is recruiting for his crew? And meanwhile we let the informers know we are interested in Waldo and the money is theirs for the best information."

Casino Auto Body was on the Boulevard. They had a fenced in lot filled with wrecks and three brightly painted tow trucks. There was activity inside the building, so they parked across the street and watched. It was close to 5:25 PM, so they waited till they closed up at 6PM. A 6Pm people began to leave the shop. They saw a single figure locking the door, that's when they exited their car. As the person was unlocking his car, Gus came up from behind him, Sean facing him spoke.

"Excuse me Sir, I'm Detective Feeney with the NYPD we would like to speak with you."

"Well I ain't got no time, so fuck off!"

Gus touched him from behind and said,

"No asshole we don't fuck off. Now he was nice to you, I won't be, so how will it be?"

"Okay, okay what do you want?"

Sean,

"Does Waldo Cammarata work here?"

The man was silent, he looked scared when Gus said.

"Either here or at the Precinct, your choice?"

"I can get in a lot of trouble."

Sean,

"I haven't asked or even know your name, just give us a simple yes or no."

You could see his brain working when he blurted out.

"No!"

"Thank you, Sir, have a nice evening."

They both pulled away from the man and walked to their car.

Sean said,

"Well we can tell Tunison old Waldo has not been truthful."

"What happens if Waldo shows up this Thursday?"

"He won't. Tunison will start his paperwork but we will get to him before parole because our gang is bigger than theirs."

Sean laughed. Gus's intuition was based on year of experience. He knew the streets but most important he knew his prey. It would take a few years for Sean to learn, but he was looking forward to it.

CHAPTER TWENTY-TWO

102nd Squad
1961

"Red this is the way I conduct my homicide investigations. This is not standard operating procedure for the NYPD but I'm using the SOP from the Los Angeles Police Department. A few years ago, I attended the FBI National Academy course for local Police and got friendly with a Detective from LA. His name was Zach Winchester and he showed me what they call a Murder Book in LA. Simply stated, it is collection of all evidence placed in a single location so as to preserve the evidence chain, enhance communication, and establish a solid case against the perp. So today we start the Murder Book on Gerard Conolly. Everything from the second we got the call, the minute we stepped into the crime scene. Includes all info be it large or small such as the name of the attendant at the parking garage to the autopsy report on Conolly's recently undigested food. Patrolman Tobias's Crime scene log is very important. I we get a tip it has to be reported, investigated and if either used or discarded it still must be entered into the book. You and I during the course of this case will separately investigate, this book keeps us together by showing where we have been, what we uncovered, and who was interviewed or involved. We both become lethal scavenger buzzards, everything is observed, everything is examined, and everything is stripped clean. Do you understand?"

"Yes."

"While we await all the autopsy, ballistic, lab and forensic reports, let's start to uncover the real Gerard Conolly."

Red started,

Gerard Conolly born July 16, 1921 Elmira, New York. Parents were Irish immigrants. Father Neal worked for the city water department. Mother Patricia stayed home. Family had six children, three boys and 3 girls. Gerard was the youngest. Honor graduate Elmira High School 1938. Graduated 1942 Colgate University cum laude. Enlisted US Army 1942. Served in Europe with the 42nd Infantry Division andcame out a First Lieutenant with a Bronze Star and Purple Heart. Attended Columbia University School of Business on the GI Bill and graduated 1946. First job Harriman Brothers as a stockbroker. Married Marilyn Whitney, a daughter of Welton Whitney (Acheson, Topeka Railroad} 1946. Marilyn had two children from a previous marriage to Charles Stimpson. Children are Cynthia, married the Viscount of Lester UK. Cynthia presently working at Bank of England. Thomas unmarried Professor at University of Michigan. Something interesting here, Conolly never adopted them and they both kept the last name Stimpson. 1956 Chief Financial Officer Harriman Brothers. 1958 left Harriman to start his own company, Gerard Conolly

Investments, 145 Wall Street. His personal worth was estimated at $10.5 million. Memberships in the Union Club, NYC and the Cos Cob Country Club. Chairman of the United Fund, Manhattan."

"The American Dream in person, yet he rents a cheap apartment in Queens and his wife knows nothing.

Gerard was very careful and secretive; this may be the reason he is dead."

Red asked,

"Can we assume that the physical evidence found in the apartment might indicate a female presence?"

"Assume is a bad and dirty word for a detective, the defense attorneys will crucify you on the stand. No, you wait for the evidence to be examined and the results finalized. Maybe that long strand of hair belongs to a guy who wore lipstick and a dress. Mr. Conolly was doing something other than a sexual tryst; this case has larger ramifications."

"What do you think?"

"It centers around his business, and his business was big money."

CHAPTER TWENTY-THREE

102nd Squad
1961

Gus's phone rang, he answered.

"Send him up."

He looked at Sean and said,

"The Street Telegraph has been transmitting our message, we have a response."

A uniformed officer came up the stairs escorting an individual and he pointed to Gus.

He was from the street, wearing a knit watch cap, mock leather black jacket, dirty jeans and Chuck Taylor hi-tops.

Gus asks,

"What's your name?"

"Boom- Boom."

"Funny you don't look like a Boom -Boom, why do they call you that?"

"If I told you I might get arrested."

"Ok Boom-Boom what do you have?"

"Where's the money?"

"Do I look stupid? You have to tell me something I do not know, then you'll get the money."

"Look Boom-Boom, that is your problem, we all take chances."

Boom-Boom sat there wringing his hands, he was sweaty and kept moving his left leg from side to side.

Sean knew the symptoms, so he gave Gus a nod and he entered the conversation.

"If it makes it easier, we will say we never heard the name Boom-Boom, or ever saw you. Is that alright?"

He stopped moving his leg and looked up and smiled.

"Yeah, that would be better."

"Do you know where Waldo is right now?"

"He's at the Roosevelt Hotel on Pitkin Avenue. My half-brother Victor went to see him, and he got on the crew."

'What's Victor's last name?"

"Lorenzo."

Gus got up and went to another phone to call for the records on Victor Lorenzo.

"Did Victor tell you where the job is?"

"No, but it is something big."

Sean got the nod from Gus, that Victor Lorenzo had a record, and motioned for Sean to let him go.

"Ok Boom-Boom you have been really helpful, if you find out anything else here is my name and phone number. Thanks."

Gus came over and placed a $50 bill on the desk. Boom-Boom grabbed it and took off.

Gus said,

"That was the best lead we got so far. Good job on getting him to talk."

Sean asks,

"Learn anything about Victor?"

"Yeah, he's a car thief. Waldo has got his driver."

"Now let's set up a surveillance of the hotel this coming Thursday, it should be easy."

"Why is that?"

"Waldo is a night animal, he hides during the day. We set up outside, he'll emerge between 9 and 10PM. Then we follow him.

"Anything else on Victor?"

"We'll be getting a photo of him tomorrow, so we will know when we see him."

"Looks like the chase is on."

CHAPTER TWENTY-FOUR

The Conolly Case
1961

The physical evidence and lab reports had arrived. For every item recovered there was a reference number and location within the crime scene. Both detectives had to use a secondary office that was normally used for meetings and spread the evidence on a long table.

Item #1 Bullet removed the body of Gerard Conolly. .45 caliber.

#2 Cigarette Stubs – One Newport filter, One Pall Mall filter. Pack of Pall Malls found in Gerard Conolly 1961 Mercedes, another pack in night table drawer at Crime Scene. Pall Mall stub found in ashtray at crime scene. The Newport Stub contained lipstick. Lipstick analyzed and identified as manufacturer Marcel Vittan Rouge Supreme color tone.

#3 Wine Glasses- contained remnants of Rothchild Maison 1931 Vintage. Only one glass had traces of lipstick and that lipstick was the above Marcel Vittan Rouge Supreme.

#4 Strand of Blonde hair. Determination that the strand is brunette, and that blond hair coloring was evident.

#5 Prescription tablets – prescribed for Gerard Conolly by a Dr. Frederick Ormsby, 345 Madison Avenue, NY, Pharmacy: Newton's 43 Toll Street, Cos Cob, CT. Tablets were called Effexor for anti- depression.

#6 Lab analysis of secreted material under victims right middle fingernail was human. A vaginal secretion that contained blood cells with the A positive blood group. Victim's blood group was B positive.

#7 Business Card belonging to victim containing the phone number 201-328-5961 written on back.

#8 Colt .45 Government Model 1911 bearing US Ordnance Corp symbol. Serial #7703621163. Magazine contained five unfired bullets. Found in hidden console of victim's 1961 Mercedes.

#9 One used condom found in victim's bedroom. Contained dried semen which was analyzed and revealed blood group B positive consistent with victim's blood type.

#10 Fingerprints- Analysis found were a set belonging to NYPD Patrolman Lawrence Russo on apartment bathroom door. Numerous prints of victim Gerard Conolly. One partial print found on bedroom headboard, unable to identify due to lack of sufficient points and smear.

#11 Bullet – retrieved from victims' body. Was of large caliber only three striations visible sent bullet to Ballistics section for comparisons.

Additional evidence returned to Investigating officers 102nd Squad.

One brown leather wallet with Brooks Brother logo containing $1000.00 in US Currency.

Five Credit cards: American Express, Diner's Club, Mastercard, Saks Fifth Avenue, and Brooks Brothers.

One Connecticut Driver's License in the name of Gerard Conolly

Parking Stub for a 1961 Mercedes Benz. Issued at Metro Parking 178th Street, Queens.

End of Evidence returned.

Red commented,

"Got a lot here Joe, where do you want me to start?"

"Red, first get the listing for the phone number written on his business card. Then check out the charges on the credit cards. Look for large dollar purchases, jewelry, couture clothing. See if he purchased airline tickets to warm locations and where he stayed. On the Diner's Club card see if there are any expensive meals during the week. And most important, who sells this expensive French lipstick that you're not going to find at the local Five and Ten."

Red laughed.

Joe smiled and said,

"You start on that and I will visit the pill doctor and run that .45 over to ballistics. I will visit Gerard Conolly Investments and see what they thought of him. Also plan on seeing some people who can help me understand Conolly's business. From now on we meet every day at start of shift to review anything we uncovered. Ok Red?"

"No other way Joe."

CHAPTER TWENTY-FIVE

Cammerata Case
1961

Hotel Rockaway, Room 342 was by all descriptions a room with no accoutrements. A single worn-down bed spring with a thin mattress, a three-drawer chest that was chipped. A table that rocked and a wooden chair that was on its last legs. The bathroom had a shower and sink circa 1938, and the toilet should have been replaced years ago. The present occupant was sleeping from a liquor induced evening. He was snoring until he woke himself up. His head throbbed so he swallowed three aspirins followed by a warm opened can of beer. He walked into the bathroom did his thing, then supported by the sink he looked into the mirror. Waldo Cammerata was not a good-looking man, he was very overweight and bald and always stared straight ahead. Combined with his six-foot five-inch frame he was menacing. The past of Waldo was behind him and he wanted it that way. He could never remember a nice day or a kind word growing up, just the heavy hand of family and society constantly knocking him down. He turned on the television and checked all five channels. Settling on soap operas and quiz shows as his daily routine until after the 6PM News. He finally got dressed. At 7:30PM he was on the telephone making arrangements for his evening soirée. Waldo had a plan and worked that plan; the days of bad decisions and actions were behind him. The nights activities of meeting, talking, screwing and planning for the score were made. His last call was to Victor Lorenzo.

"Victor pick me up at ten o'clock, I'll be in the lobby. We're going to Brooklyn."

Hanging up he went under the mattress removing a .38 Caliber Smith and Wesson revolver. Rolling up his right pant leg he placed the gun in an ankle holster. It was close to 9PM when he left the room and took the elevator to the lobby. Waving at the desk clerk he exited the hotel and went about three storefronts down to Jackie T's restaurant. Taking his usual table at the back, he had full view of those entering and leaving. Waldo was a creature of habit. Every night he ordered the same meal; a burger deluxe with French fries, large Coca Cola and a piece of apple pie. At 9:50PM he left and went back to the hotel where he sat in the lobby waiting for his ride. At about 9:55PM Victor pulled up in a black two door Chevy bearing New Jersey plates. Victor went into the hotel. About ten minutes later Victor came out followed by Waldo.

Three cars behind Victor's Gus and Sean are watching.

"Sean, run that Jersey plate."

"K-23 to Queens Central need plate information."

"Q-Central to K-23 proceed with plate number."

"K-23 needs information on New Jersey PUV789 Black Chevy."

After a about a minute,

"Q-Central to K-23, Owner Malcolm Finklestein 45 Sycamore Lane, Bogota, NJ"

"K-23 to Q Central 10-4"

"Sean, do you think Mr. Finklestein knows Victor, and let him use his car for the night?"

"No way, it has to be stolen."

"Well, we want to see where Waldo is going, not make a stolen car bust. Today is Wednesday, grab that

Knicks cap and put it in the back window. Tonight, we do not want to be bothered."

In a few seconds they were rolling and following Victor and Waldo some five cars back. After about ten minutes Sean said to Gus,

"They're heading for Brooklyn."

In another ten minutes they were on Flatbush Avenue. Victor parked the car and both men got out. They walked some hundred feet and into a bar called the Wayward Lounge. The two detectives waited and watched for two hours. At 12:40AM Waldo and Victor exited the lounge with two females. Waldo and one female got in the back seat, while the other lady cozied up to Victor in the front seat. Victor started up and headed south on Flatbush and then over the bridge into Rockaway. Red watched them turn into the large parking lot of Riis beach, He told Gus to stay on the road and enter the parking lot at another entrance where they parked and watched. Gus took out a pair of binoculars and peered through the window.

"Windows really steaming up, they're getting it on, should be over soon."

He was right for in fifteen minutes the headlights came on and the Chevy was heading back over the bridge to Brooklyn. At Flatbush and Kings Highway they stopped, and the girls got out. The Chevy sped off. Gus kept them in sight for next twenty minutes, but at a farther distance due to no visible traffic. At Utica Avenue they stopped and parked. Leaving the car, they entered a bar called the Topsy Turvy. Gus and Sean again parked and waited. About an hour later Waldo and Victor were outside with two other males.

Gus says,

"Sean, grab the camera and get some closeups."

Sean took some twenty telephoto shots of the group, getting several good closeups of the new friends. Then they broke up. Waldo and Victor went to the Chevy, while their two new fiends walked away in separate directions.

Staying on Waldo and Victor they were back in Queens. It was 4AM when they parked on Northern Boulevard went into a non-descript doorway. As Gus drove by Sean saw the sign Metropolitan Social Club, MEMBERS ONLY.

"What is this place?"

Gus explains,

A mob gathering place run by the Profaci family. Whatever Waldo is up to he needs their blessing because they will get a cut of the job."

"Why does he have to give them a cut, he's taking all the chances."

"Because they will get their cut and protect Waldo. Waldo needs their blessing and he needs their support, or he will be open to harm from others. With their blessing and support Waldo is considered a "moneymaker" for them. This recognition saves them from accepting him into their circle as a "made man", and Waldo knows that and knows they will expect more big scores. No matter how hard he tries he will always be an outside contractor. Sean, time to head back and get some sleep. Tomorrow we'll meet at 6PM and have those photos developed. Rest up me bucko, we do it all over again tonight."

Sean was dead tired, but the excitement of the job was still there, he'll be ready.

CHAPTER TWENTY-SIX
===================

Conolly Case
1961

William's appointment was with Marci Baxter, Gerard Conolly's personal secretary. As he entered the 145 Wall Street Offices he was presented with a rather austere interior. For some reason he expected statues and paintings, thick rugs and chandeliers, instead he felt he was in his dentist's reception area.

Conolly certainly did not spend his money on this place. He checked in with the receptionist who sat behind a window, and he then took a seat. About five minutes later through the door from the office side appeared a very dramatic and attractive women

"Detective Williams, nice to meet you I'm Marci Baxter."

Joe was a slightly hesitant in answering for he was red in the face. Her beauty had captured him.

"Uh, oh I'm Joe Williams, very nice to meet you."

"Let's go to the conference room, we can talk there. Will you follow me?"

"Yes, Ma'me."

Walking behind her he could not help but notice how her body moved, everything was perfect.

Reaching the conference room, they sat down. She offered up coffee, he declined.

"Ms. Baxter, please accept my condolences for the loss of Mr. Conolly."

"Thank you, he will be missed by all."

"How many persons are employed here?"

"Conolly Investments has a grand total of 45 employees. Mr. Conolly never liked large staffs. He felt that the right mix of personnel could equal the work of hundreds."

"Can you tell me if Mr. Conolly had any enemies that could have been instrumental in his death?"

A little shocked she answered,

"None, he was a kind man. A very hard worker and businessman he always found time for charitable work."

"I have to ask; did he have any affairs with other women?"

"No, definitely no. He and his wife were a loving couple."

"Ms. Baxter how long had you been Mr. Conolly's secretary?

"Seven years. He interviewed me at the first office on Church Street."

"During those seven years was there ever a time that Mr. Conolly ever seemed worried or concerned?"

"Only recently, when we merged with the new partners."

"There are partners I did not know. Who are they?

"Ronald and Roland Woodruff of the South African Woodruff Group."

"When did this partnership happen?"

"About 3 month ago."

"Why did Mr. Conolly enter into a partnership?"

"He was getting more international clients, the Woodruff Group offered more possibilities."

"Are investments the main part of this firm?"

"About 55%. With our seat on the exchange our clientele does very well."

"What's the other 45%?"

"Venture capitalism. This includes real estate investments, emerging markets and personal services."

"Conolly joined Woodruff to advance his business, why did Woodruff decide to partner?

"Mr. Conolly told me their only reason was his seat on the exchange."

"Ms. Baxter, did you know Mr. Conolly had an apartment in Queens?"

Again, she appeared shocked her mouth opened but she said nothing.

"You didn't know?"

"No, I never knew that. Is that where he was killed?"

Joe nodded yes.

"Oh my God."

"Do you want to take a break Ms. Baxter?

"No Detective."

"Ms. Baxter is it possible to get a complete listing of Mr. Conolly's clients?"

"No, that is very confidential. Ronald Woodruff would have to release that?"

"Can I see Mr. Woodruff today?"

"Let me see if I can get you in."

She picked up the phone and dialed a 2-digit number.

"HI Joyce, I'm with a Detective Williams investigating Gerard's death. He needs to see Roland today,

alright I'll wait."

While she waited, she looked at Joe and smiled.

"You can call me Marci instead of Ms., besides I'm a Miss."

Joe was happy to hear that.

"Ok Marci, nice to meet you."

They both laughed. Then she was listening to the phone.

"Tomorrow, after 3PM?"

Joe nodded yes.

"Joyce put down Detective Joe Williams for 3PM, thanks."

"Ok Joe you have an appointment. Anything else? "

"Nothing more, but if I need more information can I call you?"

"Sure, anytime."

"Well thank you Marci for meeting with me, have a nice day."

"Same to you Joe."

As he left, he could not get her out his mind. She was beautiful and for the first time he felt very comfortable in her presence, something he felt from no other woman.

Joe left 145 Wall, found a payphone and called a number.

"Office of Eli Weissman."

"Is Mr. Weissman in? Joe Williams calling."

"Please hold."

Seconds later.

"Joe, how the hell are you?"

"Good Eli, need your help, when can I see you?"

"Where are you now?"

"145 Wall."

"Great, go two blocks up Pine Street. 208 Pine, 56th Floor see you in ten minutes."

"Thanks Eli appreciate it."

The Security and Exchange Commission was the watchdog of Wall Street. Their sole purpose was to oversee the stock markets and those that worked in it and applying the needed Federal law and statues. Joe had known Eli Weissman since they were both six years old in. the Bronx. Boyhood friends they had gone thru high school together then parted for college. Joe to Fordham, Eli to Columbia. Joe trusted his friend explicitly, and now needed him to learn more about Conolly and his business. Eli was the head of the SEC New York Office and had over 600 people working for him and knew Wall Street including the sewers and those that thrived there.

Eli smiled as he came into the reception area. It was the same smile Joe remembered as a kid, one of pure joy and close friendship. Eli stood close to six and a half feet tall, his suit fit him exceptionally well, and he hugged his longtime friend.

"Been awhile buddy" said Eli.

"Great to see you" replied Joe.

Eli guided him down a long hallway to a corner office that was bigger than the squad room. The view from the office offered a grand view of the waterfront and the Statue of Liberty.

"Wow, what a view", exclaimed Joe.

"And I earned it" replied Eli.

They both laughed. Joe began by telling the story of the murder in Queens. He left out the name of the victim. When finished Eli asked,

"Great story, but what does it have to do with the Security and Exchange Commission?"

"The victim had a seat on the big exchange, his name was Gerard Conolly."

There was an immediate reaction from Eli.

"Jesus, Gerard Conolly. We have had him on our sights for years. He was very shrewd and sharp, but it was just a matter of time."

"Why was he and his company of interest to you?"

"Joe, we do random audits of firms bi-annually. His records showed a rise in foreign clientele and short time investments. To us that means he was "Parking Money", a very big infraction of the SEC statutes.

We started an ongoing case file on him about a year ago. We monitored his transactions both in and out of the country.

There was a lot of Russian and Arab money being moved, and Conolly was the mover."

"Eli what is parking money?"

"An acquiring company, let's say the Zang Corporation, a pharmaceutical giant in China wants to conceal its ownership in an attempt to complete a hostile takeover of a target company in the US, let's say Schering-Plough Pharmaceuticals. To do this they acquire all the Schering-Plough stock using a third party, in this case Gerard Conolly. Zang prepares for the hostile takeover while not disclosing certain intentions or reporting levels that will alert Schering-Plough. With money from Zang, Conolly would buy all the controlling stock and park it, until the time Zang takes it back. Conolly secures a small percentage of this transaction, usually in the high millions, and Zang takes over Schering-Plough. The other aspect is Conolly could park stock, so the money to purchase that stock could be laundered. He had a lot of clients with offshore accounts. Here your clientele are drug cartels, weapons dealers, Organized Crime, and corrupt individuals. Gerard Conolly Inc. was a service to all comers. Our last visit to Conolly was only a few weeks ago. We learned Conolly had entered into a partnership with two South Africans brothers, Roland and Ronald Woodruff of Capetown. The Woodruffs come with their own baggage of businesses. Several huge resorts and gambling casinos, three diamond mines and a uranium mine in the Congo. Own their own shipping line, Transvall Shipping, some thirty ocean freighters. They apparently have known Conolly because they are partners with him in a Grand Cayman bank. This is their first venture into Wall Street so they purchased 50% of Conolly's firm and became his partner. I said baggage before. We know from our South African counterparts the brothers Woodruff have walked a fine line between legal and illegal."

"I am going to need that data Eli?"

"I can only give you what we have and investigated. The offshore stuff will have to be from a Treasury Department unit I use. I'll get you in touch with the director, Leon Bauer. Leon knows all the players and characters."

"Thanks Eli."

"Thank me by planning on more meetings, it would be nice to see you once in a while."

Both men stood up and Eli walked Joe back to reception. They hugged each other than parted.

Joe's next visit was uptown to Conolly's doctor, Dr. Frederick Ormsby. At 345 Madison Avenue he went to the 28th floor offices and found the offices. In a few minutes he was with Dr. Ormsby. He was shocked to hear about Conolly's death. Conolly had been a patient for the past eight years, and his last appointment was about two months ago. A that appointment he complained of being anxious and could not sleep. Ormsby prescribed Effexor, with a return appointment in three months.

"Doctor, what was Effexor for?"

"For anxiety, it is a mild depressant."

"Did Mr. Conolly say anything specific about his work that was causing this condition?"

"He did come to mention that. He did say his connections were pressing for results, and he had a lot to do with little time to do it."

"Did he mention any names?"

"No, that was all he said. You know he said it like he was resigned to the fact."

"Thank you Dr. Ormsby."

CHAPTER TWENTY-SEVEN

Cammarata Case
1961

With the photos processed both Gus and Sean were into the mug books. They got lucky with an early identification on the two males that met with Waldo last night. Sean got the sheets on both men, showed Gus.

"These two are a team of strong arms. Both have served prison time. Names are Eddie LaManna and Tommy Burke. What is Waldo going to do with these two?

Gus says,

"Well he's got his driver, these two must be for holding guns and carrying out stuff. So, what is his target?"

Sean says,

"A bank?"

"No. Sean, grab his file. Where did he go to prison?"

Sean started looking and said,

"Upstate, Comstock."

"Get the Warden on the line, I have some questions."

Sean made contact with the prison, got the Warden on the line, handed the phone to Gus.

"Warden this is Detective Antaknockis 102nd Squad, NYPD. A former inmate Waldo Cammerata was recently paroled. Can you tell me anything about him, like his cell mate and friends he hung out with?"

"Detective he never gave us any problems. He hung with an all-white gang that had a prison rep of you better stay away from us. Waldo shared a cell with a long termer named Edward Leggett. They were always together, eating, talking. You know, come to remember Leggett ran that white gang."

"Do you have a full spelling of Leggett's name?"

"Just a second Detective, let me look it up. Here it is, Edward Sinclair Leggett."

"Many thanks Warden you have been a great help. Have a safe day."

"You too Detective."

Hanging up the phone Gus told Sean to run the name Edward Sinclair Leggett. Within 20 minutes he

had a file. Sean gave it to Gus. Gus went thru it very slowly.

"Mr. Leggett has an interesting history. Was in the US Air Force, worked in electric engineering. Worked for Honeywell Security Systems. Suspected in several high-end robberies and burglaries in California, Arizona, Florida, Massachusetts. Got caught, burglary of a 47th Street diamond dealer August of 1953, sentenced to twenty-five years, Comstock prison. Waldo got some good schooling."

"You think he is going for diamonds Gus?

Gus did not respond, but he stored it in the back of his mind. He looked at Sean and said,

"Maybe we'll find out more tonight, you never know."

Both detectives got in the car and were better prepared this time for a long surveillance.

Gus had brought a large thermos of coffee, a bag of doughnuts and paper cups. Sean had packed four sandwiches and carried two empty jugs for relief. It was Thursday so Gus threw the Giants cap back in the rear window.

By 9PM they were set up outside the Hotel Rockaway. Right on time Waldo was on schedule and returned to the hotel before 10PM. Again, at 10:05PM Victor went in and was followed by Waldo. Not long after Gus and Sean started up. In a few minutes they knew they were going to Brooklyn. At the entrance to the Belt Parkway they turned left and headed west. Gus grabbed a doughnut, while Sean poured him some coffee.

"They're in a rush tonight, Victor is really moving."

"Looks like they are heading for the Verrazano Bridge."

The next four miles Victor headed west on the Belt, then instead of exiting for the Bridge stayed on the Belt for five more miles. At Delevan Street they exited into the Red Hook section of Brooklyn. Making their way to Coffey Street they stopped in front of a fenced in yard. Victor blew the horn twice and the gate electrically rolled open, closing as the car passed into the yard. From the street the detectives saw a building with lights on inside. There was a sign on the fence that said, "Tooley's Bay Ship Repair".

Inside the lighted room they saw Waldo and Victor talking to another man.

Gus to Sean,

"Can you get a photo of those three with the telephoto lens?"

"Should be able to do it with this high-speed film."

Sean started taking photos, Gus got out and silently walked the street fence line. He saw another car parked inside the fence. White two door white Cadillac, he took down the plate number SPW-3802. Moving back to the car he tells Sean to finish up. Gus pulls away from the curb and parks at a cross street. Victor will have to pass them on the way out. About twenty minutes later Victor passes by and threads his way to the Belt and heading East. At Coney Island Avenue he exits. The detectives watch as he pulls into the Crown Jewel Diner. They watch them enter and sit in a booth with an unknown white male.

"Sean change out, put that leather jacket on I got in the back. Leave your gun and badge. Get a counter seat as close as you can to them and listen."

Sean made the change and walked into the diner. He found a counter chair about one booth from them.

Making no eye contact he ordered a hamburger and a coke. He could barely hear the conversation until Waldo raised his voice.

"Hey asshole Bobby Vitello spoke for you. Now are you going to do it?"

The unknown male responded by telling Waldo to keep his voice down, then the conversation reverted back to a whisper. All of sudden Victor got up, Sean tensed, and walked past on his way to the restroom. Waldo and the other guy kept talking. Then Victor returned and sat down. They kept on talking and Sean had finished his burger, now he was nursing his coke. Then they all got up and were leaving. Waldo paid the bill and they exited. Gus was taking photos of the new guy and waited for Sean. They all got in the car and Victor went south on the avenue. Sean quickly came out and got in their car.

"Did you hear anything?"

Gus was pulling out and saw Victor's car about a block ahead.

"Only once when Waldo raised his voice he said, hey asshole, Bobby Vitello spoke for you. Now are you going to do it."

"That's all?"

"Sorry that's what I was able to hear."

"Don't be sorry, you got a lot more than you know."

"What?"

"Well Bobby Vitello is a capo for the Profaci's. A recommendation from him means you are pretty good and probably a specialist. So, we got his photo and now we find out what is his expertise. I think Waldo has completed his team."

"Do we keep following?"

"Let's just see where they drop this guy off, then we'll call it a night."

Victor turned onto Avenue X in Sheepshead Bay. At 2366 Avenue X he got out and entered the address.

Victor and Waldo took off for Queens.

"Got that house number?"

"Yes."

"When we meet tomorrow develop the film and let's hope we get an ID."

CHAPTER TWENTY-EIGHT

Conolly Case
1961

Red was at his desk and on the phone with the credit card companies requesting Conolly's records for the past two months. All were accommodating and would fax him the finalized reports. He then placed a call to NYPD Communications and asked for the "Line Unit". It was answered by a recording.

"You have reached the Line Unit. After the beep record your message. Have the number ready, your name and rank, your location and the case number for this inquiry. Leave your phone number and we will get back to within twenty minutes. Thank you. BEEP"

Red proceeded to give the information required then hung up. The fax machine came on and soon credit card information came flowing in. Getting back on the phone he called the American distributor for Marcel Vittan beauty products. Dialing a number in Moonachie, New Jersey he got through to head of distribution, Pete Fortunato.

"Mr. Fortunato,this is Detective Morris Blackman of the NYPD. I am investigating a case in which we discovered trace elements of a Marcel Vittan product. Can you provide me with a listing of retailers in the metro area that sell this product?"

"First, what is the product?"

"Marcell Vittan Rouge Supreme lipstick"

"You picked the most expensive lipstick in the world. You may have lucked out because that listing is confined to only four retailers in the metro area. Are you ready to copy?

"Yes Sir, "

"B. Altman, Franklin Simon, George Van Renna, and Louis DeNobli Couture. Do you need addresses?"

"No Mr. Fortunato, you have been very helpful, thank you sir."

"Your welcome Detective Blackman."

Red then went over to the fax machine and retrieved some eighty pages of Conolly credit card purchases. As he got back to his desk his phone rang.

"Detective Blackman, Lt. Altieri of the Line Unit. We have that phone number information you requested."

"Yes Sir, go ahead."

"Area code 201-328-5961 is a private number located at 903 Garden Street, Hoboken, New Jersey listed to a P. Taylor."

"Lou, is it possible to get the phone records for the past three months?"

"Sure, you can have it in two days, give me your squad fax number."

Red gave him the number and ended the call.

Now he started separating the credit card reports. He started with Diners Club. Conolly had a zero balance. It appeared to be only meal charges. Prior to his death there were large charges at a Manhattan restaurant. The restaurant was the Bull and Bear and one day he charged a $445.00 meal. About one week later another charge of $325.00. Red looked up the location and found it in the Wall Street area.

He made a note of it. The Saks Fifth Avenue card had a zero balance with no purchases for the entire year.

Brooks Brothers card had a $12,000.00 balance. His credit limit was $20,000.00. He had made a payment of $5500.00 a month before his death. The card with the most activity was Mastercard. It appeared this was his travel only card. He had a balance of $18,000.00 with a last payment of $14,000.00. This report contained some ten pages of airline ticket purchases to Europe, the Middle East, South Korea, Singapore and South America. Checking closer he counted 25 trips to Capetown, South Africa months before his death.

Red grabbed his jacket and went downstairs to the desk sergeant who arranged for a patrol unit to drop Blackman off at the nearest subway station. He got on the D train for the ride into Manhattan. At 34th Street he got off and walked to B. Altman. Inside he asked for the store manager's office and was told it was on the third floor. He identified himself to the secretary, she made a call and he was shown into a large office. In a few minutes very busy man entered. He was impeccably dressed and had a red carnation in his lapel. He identified himself a Frederick Stuyvesant, shook hands with Red and sat down.

"What can B. Altman do for the NYPD?"

"Mr. Stuyvesant, we are investigating a homicide in Queens. Our lab teams found trace elements of a lipstick made by Marcel Vittan called Rouge Supreme. The American distributor told us only four stores sell this in the metro area, B. Altman being one of them. I would need records of sales going back four months."

"That should be easy because that one product is extremely expensive. We charge $185.00 for one tube.

If you don't mind waiting, I'll call sales inventory. He dialed a number and within five minutes a young lady appeared with a single sheet of paper, she handed it to Stuyvesant. He looked at it and handed it to Red.

There were only six entries. Four with names and credit, and two denoting cash was paid. All transactions made two months before the murder.

"Thank you very much for your assistance Mr. Stuyvesant."

He then left for Franklin Simon also on 34th Street. Again, only a small listing of sales. All credit transaction on Simon Franklin credit accounts. Next was Louis DeNobli at Madison and 62nd Street. Here he found only two cash sales over four months ago. His last place to check on was George Van Renna. This was a high-end couture house. After meeting with the manager, he was shown one credit card sale and one cash sale.

The cash sale was a week before the murder.

"Does anyone here remember this sale?"

The manager looked at the information and said the salesperson was on the floor now.

Red was introduced to Gloria.

"Gloria do you remember the person who purchase this tube of Rouge Supreme?"

"Yes, I do. She was white, about five feet five very petite, brunette and very well dressed."

Brunette rang a bell in Red's head.

"Do you remember anything else about her?"

"She spoke with an accent, it sounded German."

Red thanked her and the manager and left George Van Renna with a possible lead.

CHAPTER TWENTY-NINE

Cammareta Case
1961

Gus noted,

"The plate on the white Cadillac at Tooleys came back as registered to a Christine Vitello, 46 Underwood Road, Great Neck. So, the guy we photographed inside Tooleys was Bobby Vitello and that confirms the Profaci's are supporting Waldo. Sean who was guy they met that lived on Avenue X?"

"Named Thaddeus Zoldy, occupation welder works at Tooleys Boat Repair. He has a sheet, Burglary 1957 sent away for five got out in three."

"Where did he spend the time?"

"Comstock Prison."

"Got any more on that bust?"

"Nothing listed."

"Who was the arresting officer?"

"Detective 2nd Grade Nikkos Polezoes, 56th Squad."

"Jesus Christ! That's my first cousin's kid."

Gus picked up the phone and called the 56th Squad asking for Detective Polezoes. When he answered Gus started talking Greek. For the next ten minutes there was loud talk and a lot of laughter. Sean did not understand anything until he heard the name Thaddeus Zoldy. There was more talk in Greek then Gus hung up.

"Waldo has got himself an experienced "bar man" for his crew."

"What's a bar man?"

"If you want to hit a big vault you burn into it with a burning bar. It is a pipe filled with special alloy wire that is heated to its kindling point of 2800 degrees F. When pure oxygen is introduced into the pipe this 'burning bar' will produce a temperature in excess of 7200 degrees F and you cut through steel like butter. Zoldy is an expert with the bar. We need to hit the street telegraph and offer more money than the usual fee, and we keep following Waldo because he is ready to hit his target. Let's go see Lou, we are going to need more manpower."

CHAPTER THIRTY

Conolly Case
1961

Joe Williams had been trained to keep an investigation moving forward, so it was standard operating procedure for he and Red to discuss what they had discovered and obtained.

"Red, this lipstick trail, what have you got beside the George Van Renna lead?"

"Altmans, Franklin Simon and DeNobli hardly yielded anything. Credit card purchases were bona fide citizens. The cash purchases were a little tougher to discern, but the Van Renna lead was the most positive. Her being a brunette against our blonde hair sample from the scene had some credence. I think we should put this up on the shelf for the time being."

"I agree. Any idea who this P. Taylor from Hoboken is"

"Joe, by tomorrow we'll have phone records from 'Lines' and we will be able to see if Conolly made calls to this number from either his office, his home or the Queens apartment."

"Good, Conolly's credit purchases anything that stood out?"

"Yes, two weeks prior to his death he had two large charges at a Wall Street area restaurant, Bull and Bear. One charge was for $445 and the other for $335. He also had a large list of flights around the world. Capetown, South Africa had twenty- five visits."

"Tomorrow, I'm meeting with one of his South African partners, I'll ask about that."

"Maybe you might get a new clue"

"I hope so Red. I met with an old friend, who is head of the SEC/ NY. They were looking into Conolly for SEC violations. It seems our vic was active in moving money and assisting clients with offshore money. I got the name of a US Treasury wiz who knows where the offshore money is located. So, when I get a client listing from Gerard Conolly Investments you and I will go visit him."

"Anything else Joe?"

"That .45 automatic we found in the vic's car. I'll run it down to ballistics to have it tested. Can you call ATF with that serial number and determine if they have anything on it?"

"Ok, will do."

"I'll check out this Bull and Bear restaurant and those big purchases. Those phone records from 'Lines',

call me if something jumps out and is important."

"Will do Joe."

Williams left for the evidence room and signed out the .45 pistol. Forty minutes later he was the NYPD Ballistics Lab. He saw a familiar face.

"Jack Slater, well I'll be damned, you here now?"

"They had to find a place for me, after all I am a supporting beam of this department."

They both laughed. Slater was Joe's partner when they were on uniformed patrol.

Joe handed over the pistol.

"Need this tested, check to see if it is clean."

"Do you want to wait? Or do you want a call?"

"Call me or my partner Detective Blackman at 102nd Squad. Great to see you Jack."

"You to, Joe."

CHAPTER THIRTY-ONE

Cammerata Case
1961

Lt. Casey had met with Gus and Sean and from what they told him he agreed that more support was needed. Gus and Sean were in his office awaiting a VIP (very important policeman). Lou's reputation in the department cast a long shadow. If Casey requested assistance you responded. The office door opened and in walked a uniformed two star.

"Detectives this is Assistant Chief of Intelligence Charles Abrams. Chief, these are Detectives Antaknockis and Feeney."

They all shook hands and Abrams took a seat. He looked at Lou and said,

"Dougie, you got them pretty excited about this investigation. A chance to get a Profaci job in play doesn't happen every day, I've got SIU and ESU at your disposal, just give the word."

Lou responds,

"Charlie, not so fast. We have yet to determine the target, and when we learn what the target is, it will be a wait and see.

Right now, Cammerata has his team assembled. Bobby Vitello and the family will provide support. We need to continue watching Cammerata and his crew. To do this we are going to need your Special Investigative Unit to help us follow them round the clock. Forget about Vitello he'll be there when they split up the money, then you get him. Is that alright with you Charlie?"

"Whatever you need Dougie."

Gus spoke,

"We have another request Chief Abrams?"

"What do you need?"

"We need your "black bag" man, and a SIU team playing husband and wife tonight."

"Where?"

"Hotel Rockaway, when Waldo leaves, we want to get into his room, and we will need a diversion at the desk to get upstairs"

Abrams looked at Lou, he gave a nod.

"You got it Detective. What time you want them there?"

"Waldo is like a clock he leaves at 10:10PM. Send in the team, five minutes later we and your "specialist" walk past the desk."

Sean,

"Chief Abrams when all this goes down at the end, we want in and collar Waldo. It's our case."

"You got some smart boys here Dougie. Weren't you part of that TPF team that took down the bank robbers in the Bronx?"

"Yes Sir."

"There is no other man in this whole department that I respect more than your Lou. He will be ground commander when this thing goes down, and you will make your collar, that's my promise to you. Now you two make it happen."

Abrams stood up and left.

Gus asks,

"You know the Chief, Lou?"

"He was my partner for eight years in the 5th Squad, good man saved my ass a few times."

Meanwhile across the Squad Room.

Conolly Case

Red got a call from Ballistics.

"Is this Detective Blackman?"

"Detective Jack Slater, Ballistics Unit. Joe Williams told me to call you if we got a hit on that .45 Auto he brought in. This gun was used in two homicides. First, it is connected to a homicide in New Jersey. Homicide was in Hoboken. You will need to call a Detective Sgt. Revelli at (212)-785-5000. They had sent out an area notification that included a photo of the striation pattern. Now for the kicker, that homicide you're both are investigating in Queens, well this is the same gun that fired the fatal bullet."

"Holy Shit!"

Slater laughed.

"Tell Joe I'm sorry I gave him more work."

"Thank you, Detective Slater, we will get on it."

Red placed a call to Hoboken PD and asked for Sgt, Revelli.

"Sgt. Revelli, Homicide."

"Sgt. Revelli, I'm Detective Blackman with the 102nd Squad NYPD. We retrieved a .45 Auto in a homicide we are investigating. I just received a call from NYPD Ballistics. This pistol was the gun used in your homicide and it fired the fatal bullet in our investigation. When did your investigation start?"

"Just about two weeks ago. We responded to a shot fired and found the victim dead in the alley. It appeared the perp shot her from a car, then took off fast leaving tire marks."

"Have you identified the tread marks?"

"Yes, American Goodyear all season 16 inch."

Red knew it was not a Mercedes tire, but the coincidences of the one gun firing the bullets that killed in two separate and different cases was worth a chance question."

"Detective Revelli was your victim P. Taylor of 902 Garden Street, Hoboken?"

"How the hell did you know that? I never mentioned the name and address?"

"Taylor's phone number was found at our crime scene. The .45 Auto that killed both of our victims was in our victim's car."

Revelli responded,

"Looks like we have something in common. My partner and I will have to get together with you."

"I'll see you both tomorrow at your place at 11AM, Ok?"

"We will see you at eleven, thanks."

The phone call ended. He called Joe's pager number. Within a minutes Joe had called back.

"Red, what do you have?"

"That .45 found in Conolly's car killed a person in Hoboken, NJ by the name of P. Taylor, 902 Garden Street, Hoboken about four days before Conolly died. Now it gets better, hold on Joe. That gun also killed Conolly, the bullet taken out at autopsy was fired by that gun."

"Holy Shit!"

"My same reaction. We are meeting the Hoboken Detectives here tomorrow at 11AM.

"So, after Conolly was shot, the killer went to the garage and put the gun in the console?"

Red responded,

"We would be counting on the attendant to remember so that may be worth a chance."

Joe replied,

"That's a longshot, why don't you call the uniforms that responded? Tobias and Russo, ask them to follow up with the attendant at the garage, you have his name. Have them asked him if there was a car that drove in that night, got a claim ticket, then drove out saying they changed their mind. If the attendant remembers and he can give them a description, we may have something."

"I'll get in touch with the uniforms."

"I have an appointment with Roland Woodruff on Pine Street then I'll stop by the Bull and Bear. If anything new arises, page me."

After Joe hung up, Red got another call.

"Detective Blackman this is Agent Collins with the ATF. You requested a serial number check on a .45 Auto."

"Yes, thank you for getting back."

"Detective that was a .45 issued during World War 2. To whom we do not know. All I can tell you is that whoever used it was in the 42nd Infantry Division. We show that serial number as one of 6500 Colt 45 Auto pistols allocated to that division."

"Thank you, for your assistance Agent Collins."

As he hung up, he remembered that Conolly was a veteran of World War 2 and had served with the 42nd Infantry. He remembered his father telling him he could have kept his sidearm and brought it home, but he had enough of guns. Conolly kept his and brought it home.

Joe was on time for the meeting with Roland Woodruff, but was told Woodruff was in conference and their meeting would be twenty-five minutes later. He decided to wait. After about five minutes Marci Baxter came out.

"Hi Joe, need some company?"

"I'm usually pretty picky about who I hang around with, but in your case, welcome."

They both laughed. He liked her smile and how beautiful her large brown eyes seemed to glisten.

They talked for the next minutes and sought common interests.

Joe asked,

"Marci, since we both like the movies, would you like to see Breakfast at Tiffany's this Friday?"

"Thought you would never ask, of course I'd love to."

"Where do you live, I'll pick you up around eight, alright?"

She looked around and saw an office business card on the reception table and asked him for a pen. After writing down her address she handed it to him.

"And included is my phone number in case you have to cancel."

"Nothing on earth will make me cancel."

Her face lit up, smiling she got up, looked quickly around and planted a kiss on Joe's cheek. No more was said as she left the reception area. About five later Joe was called in and brought into Roland Woodruff's office. Seated behind the desk was a man about forty with blonde hair and blue eyes. He looked tall and was in good shape. Wearing an expensive looking gray suit, he kept his head down looking at the paperwork. Joe was standing there when he looked up and said in an authoritarian voice,

"You may be seated Detective."

He never got up from his desk, never extended his hand, just kept focusing downward at the paperwork. Joe took a seat, and then the phone rang and Woodruff picked it up. He was talking in a foreign language.

Joe thought it sounded like German. The call ended and he looked up at Joe.

"What is the purpose of this meeting? My partner has been murdered and I would think you would be trying to find his killer."

"Mr. Woodruff, I know this is an inconvenience to you, but part of our investigation is to determine if someone Mr. Conolly knew may have done him harm. A very important part of this investigation is for me to see Mr. Conolly's client list."

"That will not happen Detective. Our legal counsel has advised against that. We will require a court order to disclose that very confidential information. I think our business here is finished, good day Detective."

Joe knew better than to make a scene. He slowly got up and walked out. This asshole did not deserve the courtesy of a reply. Roland Woodruff was not his first run in with an arrogant person. Joe knew he was hiding something, and now it was unfortunate for Woodruff he had a target on his back that Joe just tacked on.

Next stop was the Bull and Bear Tavern. Joe met with the manager, Thomas Jordan. He gave him the dates of the two large Diners Club charges for Conolly. Thomas had known Gerard Conolly for over ten years and said Conolly was a great customer and friend. He would be greatly missed at the Bull and Bear.

Joe asked,

"Thomas, do you remember how many people were in his party the date he came here and spent $445.00?"

"It was only Mr. Conolly and a very pretty woman he introduced as Phyllis. They had a front table and that night the champagne flowed."

"Did you know what they were celebrating?"

"No, they never said."

"How were they when they left?"

"Very happy, but not drunk. They left arm in arm."

"Thomas did you ever see that lady again?"

"No, that was the first and last time."

"Can you tell me about the other date he came in?"

"I was on vacation that week, our assistant manager may remember. Do you need to talk to him?"

"No, not at this time."

"If I send down a Police artist, would you be able to describe her?"

"Detective, I can do you one better."

He looked over to bar, saw the person he needed and called,

"Calley, can you come over here?"

Calley was a cute lady in a short skirt. She came over to the desk.

"Detective Williams this is Calley Vincent our photographer.

"Nice to meet you Calley."

"Like wise Detective,"

Thomas spoke.

"Calley, do you maintain a file of customer photographs? Detective Williams need copies from these two dates that Gerard Conolly was here."

"Sure, give me a few minutes. I keep everything on file in the basement dark room."

She returned in a few minutes with a single folder. She pulled a photo out of Conolly and an attractive female seated at their table with champagne flutes held high.

"Yes, that is lady he brought that night" said Thomas.

Then Calley pulled out another photograph, this one with Conolly and another woman. This was taken on the date of the $335.00 charge. The woman was blonde, very attractive. She was petite and was holding Conolly's arm.

"Calley, you may have solved the case. Thank you very much. Thomas may I take these?"

"For the NYPD, our pleasure."

Joe left the tavern with the best lead to date.

CHAPTER THIRTY-TWO

Cammerata Case
1961

It is 10:15PM in the Hotel Rockaway Lobby. The desk clerk was beside himself. A few minutes prior a peaceful looking older couple came to the desk and asked for a room. As the male was signing in, the female started yelling very loudly at him. He yelled back calling her a cow then all hell broke loose. She picked up a display from atop the desk and threw it at him. He ducked but it hit the clerk in the chest and he went down behind the counter. As the older man came around the desk to help him, three men walked by unnoticed past the desk to the elevator and got on. Finally, being helped to his feet the befuddled clerk did not see the wife anywhere. The husband told the clerk he had to find her, or she would get lost and hurt. He went out the front door to the street and found her, and they both got into a car to travel back to their SIU locale.

The elevator stopped at the third floor. Gus, Sean, and the guy carrying a black bag called 'Smitty' got off. At Room 342 they listened for any inside sounds. Gus knocked on the door twice but there was no answer. 'Smitty' went to work, he opened the door in five seconds. Both detectives entered with guns drawn, the room was empty. They started searching and had scoured the entire room and bathroom finding nothing.

"Do it again. Waldo had to have written something down."

Again, they went through the wastepaper baskets finding crumpled cigarette packs, empty matchbook covers, and candy wrappers. The ashtray was full of butts. In the top set of drawers were two unopened packs of cigarettes and ten candy bars. It was Sean who found the empty matchbook cover underneath the candy bars. Every other empty match book cover was in the trash, but not this one. Sean opened it slowly and hand printed on the inside cover was '895 Bowery'. He showed it to Gus,

"Copy that address and take a photo of it. Put it exactly back where you found it. We got what we need, let's go. Smitty lock the door."

Each of them walked separately out of the elevator and passed the clerk who still looked dazed from his experience. Thanking 'Smitty' they went back to their car.

"Where to Gus?"

"To the Bowery."

It took them about twenty-five minutes. Parking on Canal Street was bad, so Gus told Sean to pull into a loading zone and placed a Mets cap in the back window. They walked up to the Bowery and saw 895 from across the street. There was no signage on the building. A very large overhead door with a driveway from the street was the main focal point. There was a front entrance single door. The building was only three stories high and looked abandoned. Gus looked up and down the street and spotted a hot dog vendor.

"What do want with your dirty water hot dog?"

"Mustard and kraut," said Sean.

"Anything to drink?"

"Coke will be good."

Gus left Sean and went up the street, in a few minutes he was back with hot dogs and sodas. They found a nearby bench and watched. It offered a great view of the building. For the next three hours they sat, talked and watched, even Gus took a short nap. An armored truck stopped and pulled up to the building. They watched as it backed into driveway, the overhead door came up and the entire truck backed in as the overhead door came back down. About a minute later another truck pulled up and parked past the driveway and stopped. Another armored truck pulled up and parked on the street. It was exactly the same as the others, all white with a red stripe on its side. No signage on the sides or a single commercial name. The overhead door opened, and the first truck pulled out and left. The second truck backed into the driveway and into the building and the door came down. The third truck moved up to the space above the driveway. Before they knew it there were seven more identical trucks parked in the street.

"Start taking plate numbers" said Gus.

They continued to watch and wait. In all they saw a total of ten trucks enter the building one at a time then leave.

Gus said,

"This the place Sean, that Waldo is going to hit. Now we have to find what's inside and when Waldo does the deed."

CHAPTER THIRTY-THREE

Conolly Case
1961

At 11AM Hoboken Detective Sgt. Revelli arrived. He was about 34 years old, just under six feet and wore a blue suit that fit him like a glove. Accompanied by a Detective Tulley they were to meet and discuss the new similarities between their cases. After all the introductions, they gathered in a conference room. Tully was carrying a box containing the plaster castes of tire tracks found at their scene. He opened the box and placed them on the table.

"These are the castes from our scene they have been identified as belonging to tires on a Ford Falcon" said Tulley.

Williams showed them the photo from the Bull and Bear. Revelli identified the woman as Phylis Taylor.

"That lady is Phylis Taylor?" asked Joe.

"Yes, Phylis, with one L, Taylor of 902 Garden Street, Hoboken, New Jersey."

Joe asks,

"Sgt. Revelli tells

"Sarge tells us who was Phylis Taylor?"

Revelli begins,

"Phylis Taylor was born April 26, 1929 in Haverstraw, NY. Daughter of Dr. Silas Taylor and wife Susan.

Graduated Vassar and the Columbia University School of Business. Married briefly to David Ripley 1950-1952, amicable divorce, no children. Former husband has been in France since 1954 as CEO of a French Shipbuilding Company, Lorient Naval. He last visited the United States in 1959. Ms. Taylor was the Chief Financial Officer for the New Jersey State Teachers Retirement Association of Englewood Cliffs. She lived alone in a seven-room apartment at 902 Garden Street, Hoboken for the past four years. Surviving her are her parents in Nashua, New Hampshire and a married sister in Wilmington, North Carolina. According to her business associates she was a very active and sharp executive with good record of investments. She had a one-million-dollar life insurance policy payable to her seven-year-old niece in North Carolina. We checked her apartment and found nothing relevant to our investigation. Checked her 1960 Chevy found nothing. She was killed on a Monday around 8PM in the underground garage of her building."

Red asks,

"Detective Sgt., in your investigation was anything found containing the name Gerard Conolly?"

"No, nothing in her apartment or car. However, we still have to check her office in Englewood Cliffs."

"Let us know if you find anything that ties her and Conolly together."

The meeting ended.

"Red, we all may discover something that ties this together."

"I know Joe, money is the key and appears the reason for these murders."

CHAPTER THIRTY-FOUR

Cammerata Case
1961

Gus and Sean were with the Lou in his office.

Casey inquires,

"Gus what did you find out in your trip to the Bowery?"

"Sean is going to do the briefing, he did a lot of work on getting this all together."

Sean starts,

"895 Bowery is owned by an LLC (Limited Liability Company) named Livingston and Thornton. They are a subsidiary of a United Kingdom firm called Boyleston Group that is headquartered in London. The Boylston Group are the primary owners of two racetracks in New Jersey, a racetrack outside of Philadelphia, a harness track in upstate New York, a NASCAR speedway in Delaware, a professional hockey team in Albany and three jai alai palaces in Connecticut. They own eight high end luxury hotels around the country of which three are in New York City. Additionally, four shopping malls all in New York State. The armored trucks we saw on the Bowery are a

Boyleston subsidiary called Strategic Transport. Their only customers are the Boyleston properties.

The principal owner and director of the Boyleston Group is a UK citizen named Billy Sands. He is a major figure in the UK organized crime circles. There is no love between Sands and the Profacis and to date no known altercations. However, Sands has made major inroads in the Canadian garbage collection business, and the Profacis fear he might move in across the border. We made an inquiry with the NYPD Organized Crime Unit who learned from their connections with the FBI and Scotland Yard that the Profacis had an invite to become a major investor of a London casino. At the last-minute Sands outbid them and from then on they had it in for Sands. Now with all of the Boyleston Groups ventures making money in and around New York, and storing the cash right under their nose, it is no wonder that the Profacis want to hit Sands where it hurts. Waldo and crew are the tools that will do it.

Gus took over the briefing.

"I contacted the NYC Buildings Department and got the existing plans for 895 Bowery. There is no alley in back of the structure nor is it connected to another building. There is a security control room on the second floor. The loading area inside has an elevator that can hold the weight of a loaded armored truck. The elevator goes down 100 feet to a vault where the trucks are unloaded, then it returns to the surface. Alternate entry is either thru the front single door or thru the roof. Either way would be easily detected and trigger alarms."

Just then there was a knock on the door and a squad detective told Gus he has a call from a SIU unit. Gus left the office and picked up the phone.

"Antaknockis"

"Detective, this is Detective Fowler with the SIU watching your suspect Cammarata. We have been on him and his crew. He entered a building on West 47th Street in the Diamond district. We followed him into the lobby of 223 W.47th. He took an elevator to the fourth floor got out, then got back in. There are six active firms on that floor, four of them diamond houses. He left the building and got back in the car with his crew. We have followed them back to the Crown Jewel Diner in Brooklyn. They all sat at a large booth had dinner for an hour, then left for Waldo's hotel where they dropped him off."

"Thanks Fowler, good work. Let me get back to you."

Gus went back to tell Lou and Sean of the phone call.

"Jesus are we on the wrong trail Gus?'" asked Sean.

"You think they got a new target?" asked the Lou.

Gus had many years of experience. He had learned from that experience. He slowly considered the new information and began to analyze the facts. The Profacis can hit a diamond house anytime, why now?

The cash in Bobby Sands' vault is bigger than a single diamond hit. No, this was a decoy move by Waldo to throw us off from the real target, 895 Bowery.

He looked at Sean.

"What is easier to fence diamonds or cold cash?"

"Cash is king."

The Lou smiled at Gus and said,

"You have trained your pupil well."

"We stay with 895 Bowery. Sean tell the SIU to stay on Lorenzo wherever he goes. Lay off of Waldo, let us give him a longer leash. We watch Lorenzo, he will always take us to Waldo and the rest."

CHAPTER THIRTY-FIVE

Conolly Case
1961

The US Treasury Department NYC Offices occupied four floors of the Federal Building on Church Street.

Joe and Red arrived to meet with Director Leon Bauer.

Joe opened with,

"Eli spoke very highly of you Leon. He believes you may be of some help to us in our investigation."

"Well Eli is a special person, if he sent you then you can be trusted. I am very familiar with your victim Gerard Conolly, let us say he was a person of interest. About three years ago we were investigating a member of a NY mob family."

'Which family did they belong to?"

"The Bonanos, this wise guy was an underboss and he was skimming profits from the family bookmaking operations in Brooklyn and Queens. He had taken some $5.5 Million and placed it in a Grand Cayman Island bank.

"How did you get the lead on this?" asked Joe.

From his wife's income tax statement. She owned a dog grooming business in Brooklyn, but her numbers were really overboard for that type of business. We got warrants and got into her U.S. accounts and found all of this money was transferred to a Grand Cayman bank. Needless to say, we and the FBI

were able to get a witness against the family. The wise guy and his wife are now safely living in the witness protection program. Now for your victim Conolly. In order for us to get the Grand Cayman account information we needed Scotland Yard since Grand Cayman is a British Commonwealth member. And we got an added prize. Gerard Conolly's firm had some $20 Million in the bank. We started an investigation on taxes not paid, when all of sudden the account was closed with one big transfer."

"When was this transfer?" asked Red.

Bauer got up from his chair and went to a file cabinet. He came out with a blue colored folder, he opened it and said,

"June 11 of this year. All funds transferred to the Bank of the Transvall, Capetown, South Africa."

"That was one day after Conolly was killed." said Joe

"Is there a name on that South African account?" asked Red.

"What do you know about the Woodruff Brothers?" asked Bauer.

Joe replied,

"Only that that they own huge parcels of land throughout South Africa, two diamond mines and an ocean shipping line called Transvall Marine. Main headquarters is in Capetown. Mr. Roland Woodruff is an arrogant man who is hiding something. My meeting with him was not fruitful."

Bauer continued,

"The other brother is the same and stays in the background, while Roland is the public face. For years in some cases they have walked the narrow line from smuggling, fraud, and maybe murder. Conolly needed them for international exposure, they need him for his seat on the exchange. The Conolly money that was transferred to the Woodruffs, Conolly must have stolen it from them and they made sure they got it back."

"Leon it was a great pleasure meeting you." said Joe.

"The pleasure was mine, give my best to Eli."

CHAPTER THIRTY-SIX

The Lou Monthly Meeting
1961

Lt. Doug Casey was a cop's cop. He was highly respected amongst his peers and charges. He was not a hands-off commander, who delegated everything except his political /social calendar. One of the things he had learned from some of his more successful bosses was that as the boss you had to know what your people were doing. At the end of every month Casey would meet with each of his seven teams and be briefed on how their cases were going. Casey never wanted to be called in on the carpet by a brass star and not know what was going on. Byron Crandall, the supervisor of a squad he was one of the best Squad Sergeants in the Department. Crandall could command a squad with his eyes blindfolded. Now with both of them listening to the monthly re-hash, the monthly ritual began. First in were Antaknockis and Feeney.

Sean began reciting everything they had to date including Waldo's trip to 47th Street.

Lou asked,

" Both of you are certain the hit will be the Bowery versus the Diamond district?"

"More than certain Lou." said Gus.

"Explain your reasoning?" asked Sgt. Crandall.

"The Profaci's have it in for Bobby Sands. They are the sponsors of this show. They want to hurt him where it hurts, and as far as we know he has no interests in diamonds." said Sean.

"Does Waldo know he is being watched?"

Gus responds,

"Lou, he wouldn't be Waldo if he didn't think we were watching, but so far there is no indication by him that he senses a surveillance. From the first day we got onto him he has yet to try and slip away, he just continues on doing his business Lou."

Sean reports,

"I speak to the SIU teams daily, they say he is not aware of them."

"Ok, looks like you're both on top of this. Get out of here, send in Williams and Blackman."

Joe and Red take their seats.

"What have you two got so far?" asked Crandall.

Joe says,

"We know Conolly was playing with client's money. He was parking money for use elsewhere. In this case a Grand Cayman account, however his South African partners took it all, the day after he was killed."

Red suggests,

"There is a connection with this Phylis Taylor murder in Hoboken. Same gun was used in both cases. We do not think Conolly killed her but it was made to look that way. Hoboken detectives will be searching her workplace. We are trying to determine if there was relationship here. So far all we have is a photo of Conolly and Taylor at a Wall Street tavern."

"Joe what do you think?" asked Lou.

"Big money and lots of it. The info on the closing of and the full transfer of money the day after Conolly was killed is significant."

"Why do you say significant?" asked Crandall .

"It says a lot about the state of relations between Conolly and the Woodruffs. Did they suspect him of swindling them, did they decide to end the partnership?"

"What's your plan here?" asked Lou.

"If we get lucky and the Hoboken guys are able to find a connection between Taylor and Conolly we may be able to figure out how much Conolly was going to stow away from the Woodruffs. Also, we have not ruled Conolly's wife."

"Why the wife?" asked Lou.

Red reponds,

The gun that killed Phylis Taylor was a war souvenir of Conolly's. It was also used to kill Conolly. It was left and found in Conolly's car to throw us off. We believe the gun was kept somewhere in Conolly's Cos Cob home. It was stored there and forgotten, and only a few people knew of it. We need to talk to the staff of the house; they usually know more than anyone."

Crandall asks,

"Who killed Conolly in his Queens apartment, the wife?"

"No Sarge, The Woodruffs planned it, but brought in a highly paid gun to do the deed."

"Who and where is this assassin?" asked Lou.

Joe replied,

"A very attractive female. She was pictured with the victim in the photo from the second dinner at the Wall Street tavern. We know she was blonde at the time, smoked Newport cigarettes. She wore a very expensive French lipstick and speaks with an accent described as German. She did the job and has since returned to her home base."

Red continues,

"We believe that she may have been introduced to our victim at his office by Ronald Woodruff. Conolly took one look and his testosterone took over from there."

Crandall asks,

"When will you get some sort of confirmation on all this?"

Joe answers,

"As soon as we get something from Hoboken that will tie in Taylor to Conolly. We also have to go back to the office and interview Conolly's secretary Marci Baxter. She may be the only person who can Identify this blonde assassin."

Lou says,

"Okay you two continue with what you got and keep me informed. Send in Mason and Burrows."

CHAPTER THIRTY-SEVEN

Conolly Case
1961

Joe Williams met Quentin Dawes and his wife Sarah at the Philo Day's Café on East Putnam Street in Cos Cob. Joe had asked a Cos Cob detective to arrange the meeting. Quentin Dawes was Gerard Conolly's butler for the past eight years and his wife Sarah the head maid. Joe needed to speak to people who knew Conolly and his domestic situation.

Joe spoke,

"I appreciate you meeting with me Mr. and Mrs. Dawes. As you know my partner and I have been investigating Mr. Conolly's murder for the past month. I have come with questions that need to be answered. Did Mr. Conolly own a gun?"

"Yes, he did. It was a sidearm from the war, Colt.45 Automatic", said Quentin.

"Do you know where he kept it?"

"In the bottom drawer of his wardrobe" replied Sarah.

'When was the last time you saw it Sarah?"

"About three months ago. I was putting in some sweaters. It was there in the holster."

"Have you seen it since?"

"No, that was the last time."

"Who else knew about the gun?"

"I would think Mrs. Conolly knew."

"We all know Mr. Conolly travelled extensively and was away for long periods of time. Did Mrs. Conolly ever entertain guests when he was away?"

They both looked shocked that he would ask such a question.

Quentin replied,

"Detective Williams, an important part of our job is discretion. We would be violating the trust we have been given by the Connolly's."

"I know that trust and honor are very sacred to both of you, but a man was murdered, a man you knew and served. The apprehension of his murderer takes precedence over these rules. Can you provide me with something?"

Both were quiet, and hesitantly looked at each other. Then Sarah spoke.

"The Mrs. was having an affair with Roland Woodruff."

"How long was this going on?"

"It started a year ago. Mr. Conolly would be gone, Woodruff would show up and stay over for a few days." said Quentin.

"Were they intimate?"

Again, the hesitancy, Quentin replied.

"Yes, they were very intimate, very obvious."

"Before Mr. Conolly was murdered, he was on trip to South Africa. Do you remember if Woodruff was here?"

"He was here for four days." said Sarah.

"I know this has been very painful and difficult for both of you. This will all be kept confidential. You have answered what we needed to know. Thank you both."

Meanwhile in Hoboken, NJ

Red was at Hoboken Police Headquarters meeting with Revelli and Tulley.

Revelli spoke,

"The search warrant was signed yesterday; we went in this morning and searched Ms. Taylor's computer and files. Detective Tulley went thru everything an found this. Ms. Taylor had the full responsibility for all portfolio investments of the association. She had the authority to seek out potential high yielding portfolios that return long end stability and profit. Five months ago she received an investment prospectus from Gerard Conolly that totaled some $500 Million. Everything was set for the purchase of these portfolios but was stopped two days before she was murdered."

"What was reason for not proceeding with this purchase?" asked Red.

Tulley replied,

"There was a side note in her business diary:

.... "Conolly silent partners have bad baggage, cease all future plans and meetings".....

"Anything to determine how she got this information and from where?"

Tulley replied,

"Nothing, but everything stopped that day. Phone records were checked and there must have been some twenty calls to her phone coming from Conolly's office."

Revelli spoke,

"Looks like she did some due diligence, got the hard facts and killed the deal."

Red added,

"So, she was killed for not going through with this investment, but Conolly had to know this would happen."

"Well his partners had other plans" said Revelli.

It took Red about an hour to get back to the squad. As he entered the squad room he saw Officers Tobias and Russo waiting for him.

"Hi guys, got anything from that parking lot attendant?"

"Sure do" said Russo.

Tobias reported,

"Detective we asked him if he remembered a car coming in, grabbing a ticket, going up into the garage then coming back and saying they changed their mind. He did remember a very pretty lady doing just that. He said about a little after midnight a white Ford Falcon came in driven by a woman. She drove up the ramp and was maybe up there for five minutes, then came down and said she changed her mind about parking there."

"Did you get a description from him?"

"Yes. Female white, blonde hair, very pretty and had an accent. Says it sounded like German"

"Tobias, if I give you a photograph, could you show it to him and see if she was the same lady?"

"Will do Detective."

"Thanks guys you have been a great help.

As they left Red sat down and started thinking. She had just murdered Conolly and was returning the pistol to his car. She was doing her job quite well but not that well. She now made a mistake. The attendant had said she was driving a Ford Falcon, the tires castes from the Hoboken murder scene were from a Ford Falcon. Where did she get the car from? Did she steal it? Did she rent it? Red got on the phone and called Records.

"This is Detective Blackman 102nd Squad. I need any records of Ford Falcons stolen between these dates anywhere in the city. Need ASAP, thanks."

He looked across from his desk and saw Sgt. Crandall in his office. He got up and knocked on the door frame. Crandall looked up.

"What's up Bagels?"

"Sarge, I need a look up of car rentals in the city and I haven't got the time to go to each rental company.

Is there a source that can give me an answer?"

"Call Police Headquarters, extension 1544. Asked for Lt. Kat Simmons, if she gives you a problem use my name."

"Thanks."

He placed the call to the headquarters, put in the extension and it was answered.

"IBM Unit."

"Lt. Kat Simmons please."

"Yes, Lt. Simmons speaking."

It was a very light female voice.

"My name is Detective Morris Blackman 102nd Squad, I was referred to your unit for a lookup on car rentals in the city. I have the dates and am particularly looking for a Ford Falcon rental. Can you help me out?"

"Detective, this unit is an experimental testing site for the NYPD. We are seeking ways to institute computerization into the workings of the department. Right now, the high brass view us as a waste of money and time. This unit consists of me and two tech aides and I am sorry to tell you, even if we could I have been told we are to stay out of everything from A to Z."

"What about Homicide?"

"Unfortunately, even that."

"Lieutenant Simmons I need this information, so my Sergeant told me use his name if I encountered a problem. Sergeant Byron Crandall is his name."

There was silence on the other end. She came back on.

"Give me your request and your office number."

Red gave her the request and she hung up.

He went back over to Sgt. Crandall.

"Thanks, Sarge, I got thru to that number. That female Lieutenant was kind of loopy. First, she's telling me there is no way she can help, then I mention your name and she takes my request. Do you know her?"

Crandall smiled,

"My ex-wife. Married to her for ten years, then the job took its toll on both of us, we parted on good terms. Every Christmas we see each other. She's a graduate of Princeton, extremely intelligent and a good cop. You married Blackman?"

"No, haven 't even thought about it."

"Keep it that way. When that special lady comes along, you'll know. It takes a special woman to be married to a cop."

"Thanks, Sarge."

CHAPTER THIRTY-EIGHT

The Cammerata Case
1961

Saturday night Victor Lorenzo was on the move in a stolen four-door blue 1961 Dodge Polara. At the Rockaway he picked up Waldo. Waldo was carrying a small canvas tool bag by the straps. Driving about eight blocks he dropped him off at a taxi stand. Waldo got into a yellow cab and took off north, while Victor continued down the boulevard making three pickups. Each crew member was wearing a backpack. The SIU followers knew something was quite different tonight, so the radios were blaring out calls for extra units and the two detectives of the 102nd Squad. One SIU team followed Victor's Dodge into Manhattan. Waldo's yellow cab was picked up before the Manhattan Bridge. All SIU units radioed in their locations. Gus and Sean got the call and were enroute to Manhattan. In about twenty minutes everyone was in the Bowery area. Then the shit hit the proverbial fan. Waldo got out of his cab and ran into a parking garage. The SIU team followed but Waldo was fast this day, and he disappeared. Lorenzo stopped the car and the three crew members exited in three separate directions. Victor continue to drive about three more blocks then parked in an underground garage. By the time the SIU got there he was gone and out of site.

For the next thirty minutes the area was deluged with units, but the fact was that Waldo and his crew had vanished. Gus and Sean arrived and were told the bad news. Both partners separated and checked underground garages but found nothing. Gus initiated the next move.

"Have everyone hang around 895 Bowery, they have to come out and that seems like a good place. Don't make a big scene, everybody stay in touch."

When Waldo bolted from his cab and ran into the parking garage, he only went down two levels. Looking for level 2 space 209, he found the doorway. Opening the door and immediately shutting it he now climbed down a ladder some 75 feet below the street surface. At the bottom of the landing was another door which opened onto a double set of rail tracks. He pulled out a flashlight and compass. Pointed himself in the direction of NorthNorEast and started walking. The other three crew member had all gone down into the subway. Each of them took out their compasses and headed to the ends of their respective platforms and followed the compasses EastSouthEast. Once in the subway tunnels each one looked for a lighted sign that said 'DWN75'. Each one opened the door and like Waldo climbed down a ladder 75 feet to a door that led to a double rail track. Victor had it the easiest. He parked the Dodge on level 6. He got out his flashlight and compass and walked to space 67. He opened the door and climbed down some 50 feet where he found the double rails. On a compass reading of SouthSouEast he turned on his flashlight and started walking. Soon they all converged at a given point underground. They had all found the abandoned subway line and now were near their target. Walking all together with Waldo in the lead, their flashlights illuminated a Con Edison Chevy Pickup fitted with a railroad wheel attachment. The truck was parked on the tracks near a large orange x painted on the subway wall. Next to the wall were 2 large acetylene tanks, 2 large oxygen tanks. In the truck were some very large carbon dioxide fire extinguishers, the 'burning bar' and all sorts of hammers and picks. All pre-positioned by the family Profaci. Waldo pointed to the orange x and Burke and LaManna were soon banging away with sledgehammers. After twenty minutes they had produced a hole big enough for two men to walk through. Waldo entered first and was facing a sheetrock wall. He knew behind that wall was an elevator shaft to the underground vault. Now Waldo would put his electrical and electronic skills he had learned in prison. Seeing the electrical box mounted on the wall he went to work. He rewired the alarm system to a small box he carried. This rewiring showed the system as armed, but in fact there would be no alarm. He found three wires and with alligator clips that he attached to another box that would send the video picture of the vault into a never-ending loop. Upstairs in the security control the on-duty operator did not notice the flicker, instead he saw a recording of the same picture he had been watching all night. Waldo gave the nod that all was clear. Lamanna took a compass saw and cut a large circle through the sheetrock into the elevator shaft. Waldo touched some wires together and there was a noise of machinery running, the elevator was slowly coming down. He told LaManna to alert him when the elevator was even with the sheetrock hole. LaManna called out and Waldo stopped the elevator. Burke expanded the hole with a sledgehammer. Now they moved all the equipment from the subway tracks and the truck through the walls onto the elevator. When all was loaded, Waldo opened the elevator panel and slowly controlled the descent to the vault. It was now about 3AM Sunday morning. Waldo had planned it would be another fourteen hours before they could leave with the loot.

CHAPTER THIRTY-NINE

Conolly Case
1961

Red was on the phone with Leon Bauer at Treasury. Joe was arranging a lunch meeting with Marci Baxter.

Joe said,

"Great, I'll meet you at Bradshaws at 12:30PM tomorrow, anxious to see you and thank you."

He looked to see Red writing on a pad with the phone to his ear. He soon finished and saw Joe waiting.

Red spoke,

"You were right to call Bauer, he had some updated information regarding Conolly/Taylor.

It seems five weeks before Taylor was murdered she and Conolly opened a joint account in the Bank of Aruba under the trade name Spinnaker Limited."

Joe commented,

"So, both were going to play with the NJ Teachers Fund?"

"Seems that was the case, but two weeks later she withdrew from Spinnaker, took all the money and closed the account."

"Well that makes sense with what she wrote in her records about Conolly's partners, but why was she killed?"

"Maybe it was that she opened a new account with the Royal Bank of Barbados under the company name Wellesley Partners listing her as the only principal."

Joe responded,

"Jesus, besides screwing Conolly, she was going through with the deed on her own."

"Looks like that. She used Conolly to teach her how it was done, then dropped him to go on her own."

Red replied,

The brothers Woodruff knew Conolly was going to screw them, so they got him first. However, they needed to negotiate with Taylor and win her over just like Conolly did, then she would invest with them, and then they could steal it. But her pulling out of the deal changed things. They decided to kill her and deal with her successor, it would be easier that way. We know someone killed Conolly in his apartment. Connolly's gun killed Taylor because Roland Woodruff took it while romancing the widow Conolly and passed it on to his paid assassin for the hit."

"Have an idea who this paid assassin is?" asked Joe.

"Just what we got so far, the assassin is a female, attractive because Conolly bedded her, speaks with a slight German accent, and wears that expensive lipstick."

"You know Red for a rookie Detective you're pretty good at this but remember I'm your trainer so make sure I get some credit."

"I'll tell Lou you're a genius, and he better watch out or you will take his job."

They both laughed

CHAPTER FORTY

Cammeratta Case
1961

Waldo and crew had worked hard for some seven straight hours. The vault was well made, but it could be defeated. Still on schedule they had some five hours left before the daily vault operations would begin. Thaddeus Zoldy dressed head to toe in an asbestos fire suit was pushing the burning bar further into the vault lock mechanism, LaManna and Burke using the fire extinguishers kept the rest of the room from igniting. Waldo looked at his watch, they were ahead of schedule.

On the street outside Gus and Sean debated to go in, and alert the Security control operator that the place was being robbed. If they did, it would be a partial victory for they needed to catch Waldo and the Profacis red handed.

Gus says,

"They just vanished as if the earth swallowed them up, they could be anywhere. Sitting here we will never know where they plan to exit."

Just then it hit Sean he knew somebody who would know. He ran to a street phone and dialed a number.

A female voice answered,

"Hello."

"Mom, is pop there? I have to talk to him."

A few seconds later,

"Yes Sean, what do you need?"

"Pop, I'm at 895 Bowery sitting on a major robbery in progress. We were following this crew when they

all scattered and disappeared underground."

"Sean, what's the closest cross street?"

"Corner of Bowery and Prince Street."

For the next minute there was a silence on the other end, Sean got worried.

"Pop you still there?"

"I know the area, just give me a few more seconds. Closer to a minute went by when Tim Feeney came back online.

"Sean, the old Nassau subway line once ran under that area. The trains that ran were the BB, GG, KK, and the TT. Prince and Bowery was a major stop. The whole line was shut down in 1957, but the tracks and stations are still there. The Nassau Line was one of the deepest excavated rail lines. Now everything runs on top of it."

"If you needed to haul out a lot of money out from that location and get up to the street, how would you do it?"

The older Feeney again thought for a few seconds then replied.

"I would use the tracks. Pack the money onto a track vehicle and head toward the Manhattan Bridge."

'You mean go over the bridge to Brooklyn?"

"No, stop short of the bridge, and take another closed down Nassau Line tunnel that will bring you further north. This tunnel will take you to the abandoned Nassau Line shops. This is where trains were fixed and repaired, it was huge. There, all the maintenance people took a truck ramp up to the street level."

"What streets were near this ramp?"

"Houston and Columbia Streets right at the corner. They had a big fenced in lot for parking, probably have public housing there now."

"Pop thanks, if this goes down and we get them, you're getting a steak dinner at Peter Luger's"

Sean hung up and went straight to Gus.

"Partner now is the time to be patient, I know where they will surface."

"What do you know?" asked Gus.

"I know we have to get everyone up to Houston and Columbia Streets. Call the Lou tell him to meet us there so he can set up his operation. As my senior, I suggest you leave an ESU unit and two patrol cars here just in case I'm wrong and they walk out the front of this place."

"That's re-assuring. Okay kid I hope your right."

CHAPTER FORTY-ONE

Conolly Case
1961

Bradshaw's was a nice place to meet for lunch. The menu was good, and the ambience was modern.

Marci Baxter was an attractive woman who moved with a certain grace that exuded beauty as she neared the table. Joe stood up and gave her a kiss, she smiled.

"You look beautiful" said Joe.

"Thanks, you're not bad yourself."

Since the movie date, things had sped up between the two. He yearned to be near her, and she found him very attractive.

"Marci, I hope you don't mind but our investigation at this point needs some facts verified and you may be an important witness, so before I start let's have a drink to us."

She smiled as the waiter as if on cue brought her favorite, a Manhattan while Joe had Bushmills on ice.

Toasting the occasion, they both knew they were in love with each other. Joe had been a bachelor far too long and had met his share of women, but this one was very special.

"Alright Detective Williams fire away."

"We've come up with the murder weapon. It was used to kill Conolly and a female named Phylis Taylor.

Did you ever hear that name mentioned?"

"No."

"Here is a photo of her with Conolly. Could you have seen her using a different name?

"No, I never saw that person."

"She was murdered two days before Conolly was killed. The gun the killer used belonged to Conolly."

"Oh my God, your telling me he killed this lady."

"No, he didn't but someone else did. Marci, can you remember if Conolly was introduced to or met someone while at the office."

She took a sip of her drink and thought quietly for a minute.

"I do remember a person Roland brought over to meet Gerard. She was a female auditor from the Capetown office who would be in the city for a week."

"Anything important required and audit?"

"No, but the next day she and Conolly were having lunch at a fancy place."

Joe went to his folder and pulled out the photo from Conolly's second time at the Bull and Bear.

"Is this that person?"

"Yes, that is the auditor."

"Remember her name?"

"Julia Van Niekerk."

"Tell me more about her?"

"She was very pretty and very well dressed. Had blonde hair, not her natural color. She also spoke with an accent."

"The accent sounded like German?"

"No, I know what German sounds like. Her accent was Afrikaans, same as Roland Woodruff."

That got Joe's attention.

"You're doing great Marci. Is there anything else that you remember about Ms. Van Niekerk, anything no matter how minor?"

"Well I complimented her on her lipstick. It was the most beautiful shade of red I had ever seen. She told me the name of that shade; it was called Rouge Supreme."

"Did you ever hear of it before?"

"No, but I looked it up. It is made in France by Marcell Vittan, and very expensive."

Joe smiled.

"How many times after that did you see her in the office?"

"Joe, I don't think I ever saw her again."

"Marci, you would make a great detective, your help is much appreciated, and personally I really enjoyed interviewing you."

Marci did not answer when she thought of something else.

"Joe, this may not be connected to your case, but during this time I went out to lunch with Joyce, she's Roland's secretary. She thought Roland was having marital problems back home. She mentioned he was dealing with a Private Investigator."

This perked up Joe.

"Did she mention the investigator's name?"

She thought for a moment.

"Something like Murdock."

Joe had to leave and get back to Red.

"I love you Marci Baxter, thank you for coming into my life."

They kissed and parted, both enjoying their time together.

When Joe got back to the Squad, he told Red of the positive identification by Marci and that they needed to contact the FBI for international help regarding Julia Van Niekerk. Just for the hell of it he went to the yellow pages of Manhattan and looked up Private Investigators, there was a Raleigh Murdock listed as a fiscal investigator at a Wall Street address not far from the Woodruff office. He and Red would pay him a visit.

Red got in touch with the international section of the FBI in Washington, DC. And spoke with Special Agent Andrea Alvarez.

"Julia Van Niekerk is a person of interest in two homicides in the United States. The following description; Female, White, petite in size, speaks Afrikaans. I am forwarding by fax a photo of here taken about a month ago. Any help you can give us will be appreciated."

"Detective I will first forward this our contacts in the South African National Police and Interpol.

If any agency identifies or locates her, they will contact you direct."

"Thank you, Agent Alvarez."

Joe motioned that he was heading for the car. In about two minutes Red was in the car heading for Wall Street. They arrived at 965 Wall Street and took the elevator to the 21st floor of Raleigh Murdock Investigations. Inside they found a modern well-furnished office. Identifying themselves they were

ushered into a large corner office. Murdock was dressed in an expensive three-piece suit. He looked to be in his fifties, and in good shape.

"How can I help you Detectives?"

"Mr. Murdock did you ever do work for Roland Woodruff? "asked Joe

"That is confidential information, you'll need a court order."

"Not when inquiring about a homicide."

"Who was murdered? Woodruff?"

"No, his partner Conolly."

Murdock opened his mouth and was turning white, then he said,

"Oh Jesus, he killed him over that?"

"Apparently he did. And to clarify your statement that person was Roland Woodruff?

Murdock was running his fingers through his hair. He looked up and said,

"Yes."

Red asked,

"Mr. Murdock what did you uncover for Mr. Woodruff that would account for Conolly's murder?"

"I'm a former Treasury Agent who has a knack for finding hidden money. Woodruff heard of my reputation and hired me to trail Conolly and his money. I hit gold in Aruba. Conolly and a friend had opened an account under the name Spinnaker

Limited. I reported that to Woodruff, he paid me and that was it."

"Does the name Phylis Taylor ring a bell Mr. Murdock?

"Yes, she was Conolly's friend, the other half of Spinnaker."

"Well she was murdered about 2 days before Conolly."

Murdock put his face in his hands.

"Oh God no."

"Mr. Murdock you're to come with us, we will need your statement in writing. You're not being arrested we just need your signed statement" said Red.

Murdock got up from his chair and accompanied both Detectives on the trip to the Precinct.

CHAPTER FORTY-TWO

Cammaratta Case
1961

Zoldy turned the knob on the gas line and the bar fizzled to a stop. He took off his asbestos hood turned to Waldo and said,

"She's ready to be opened."

Waldo walked up to the smoldering door and placed a four-foot-long cold chisel against the exposed pins. In his other hand he had an eight-pound sledgehammer. With the expertise of a diamond cutter he hit the chisel head once and the pin receded opening the door very slowly. LaManna and Burke grabbed the door and pulled it open. They all entered and stood silently staring at all the money atop three long tables. All the piles were equal in height. Waldo counted one pile.

"That's a million-dollar stack. Now start counting the other stacks."

LaManna started where Waldo left off, Burke started counting the other table, while Lorenzo chose the last table.

LaManna said,

"I got thirty million on this table, that includes your single stack Waldo."

Burke responded,

"Same here, thirty million bucks."

Lorenzo added,

"Another thirty million."

Waldo tells them,

"Lorenzo, break out the duffel bags. Tell me how much you can get into one bag. Start now."

Lorenzo took about three minutes and when he closed the bag, he told Waldo,

"It's full at ten million."

"Ok guys we fill up eight more bags and we are gone. Zoldy wipe down all the tools for prints and leave everything here. The elevator will be loaded with us and nine duffle bags. We do it in one trip and we are out of here in thirty minutes."

Waldo was running the numbers through his head. Ninety million dollars was a great haul, but the Profaci's would get their cut first and that would be fifty-five million dollars, leaving Waldo and crew thirty- five million dollars. That was the way of the mob. They provided support, you did the hard work and they still got the bigger share. Waldo shivered at the thought of trying to screw them. Soon nine filled duffel bags were on the elevator along with the crew. It stopped at the area where the holes were in the walls. Everyone helped with the bags as they were loaded in the bed of the Con Ed pickup truck. Lorenzo found the keys on the visor and started the engine. Waldo got into the front passenger seat and pulled a map out of his tool bag. Told Lorenzo to make sure the track wheels were engaged to the track. Lorenz gave the thumbs up sign and they took off with LaManna, Zoldy, and Burke sitting in the back seat. At about thirty miles per hour and headlights on they proceeded through the dark underground tunnel. Waldo saw daylight ahead of the pickup and told Lorenzo to slow down. He turned on his flashlight and looked at his map. He was looking for a side marker that said NLT56. Telling Lorenzo to slow down he saw the marker and then told him to stop.

"Burke, get out and throw that switch."

Burke left the pickup and ran up to the switch. He unlocked the handle and moved it 180 degrees to the right then relocked it. Lorenzo moved the pickup forward and Burke got back in. As it approached the switch, the tracks moved the entire pickup to a loop that entered another tunnel and Lorenzo resumed his thirty miles per hour speed. It took them ten minutes to reach the end of a line and arrive in the abandoned maintenance yard. The yard was huge and was lit by the incoming morning light seventy feet straight up. Waldo looked around and saw the truck ramp, their escape route to the street surface.

Waldo told Lorenzo to raise the railroad wheels which forced the pickup off the rails and onto level ground. Waldo got out and said,

"Everyone stay here, I have to make a call. Zoldy, you still got that bolt cutter?"

"Yeah, right here."

"Come with me, I'll need some locks busted."

Both Waldo and Zoldy started walking up the large truck ramp. At the top was a large overhead door that was chain padlocked to the wall. Zoldy cut it off and they raised the door. Now outside in the large fenced in parking lot Zoldy again cut off a padlock on a fenced gate.

"Stay here, I will be right back" said Waldo.

Waldo walked across Columbia Street then up to corner of Houston Street. He found a payphone in front of a pharmacy and made his call. It only took a few seconds, he hung up and walked back to Zoldy.

"Just close the gate no lock up needed."

They returned to the underground yard and waited with the rest of the crew.

From a roof of a building on Columbia Street overlooking the fenced in parking lot.

"Now what was that all about?" asked Sean.

"The Profacis are coming for their money. It seems my young pupil we will be witness to a huge takedown. We need to prepare the arrest scene, time to call Lou."

Sean got on the radio and requested Lt. Casey. Casey came on and said,

"All unit's changeover to K Channel 9"

With this in place everyone involved would be in touch on a separate channel that was restricted to this particular operation. Sean briefed him on the present situation. Casey told him to remain in place and report. He announced over the network,

"Command post K-61 now active, all units check in?"

"Chief 22 on-line." Chief Abrams responded.

"Highway 3 and 6 on-line."

"ESU Truck 67, ESU Truck 68, ESU TRUCK 72, and ESU Truck 101 on-line."

"Patrol unit 33, Patrol Unit 37, Patrol Unit 51, Patrol Unit 54 on-line"

"K61 receives all. Will advise when to move."

CHAPTER FORTY-THREE

Conolly Case
1961

Joe and Red were drinking their coffee when the call came in from Johannesburg. Previously they had been notified by Special Agent Alvarez that an Interpol Inspector named Mahlan had called in that they were involved with a person of interest using the name Julia Van Niekerk. Red picked up the phone.

"Detective Blackman, 102nd Squad."

"Detective this is Ben Mahlan of Interpol, I am responding to the inquiry Agent Alvarez published.

"Yes Inspector, many thanks for the call. My partner Joe Williams is now on an extension so we can have a three-way conversation."

"Hello, Detective Williams."

"Hello Inspector Mahlan."

Alright gentlemen, tell me what you have so far in your case, so I can see if we can help you."

Joe started and told about the initial murder of Conolly in Queens and the evidence they collected,

Van Niekerk's meeting with Woodruff, then the Taylor murder, followed by the identification of Van Niekerk by Marci Baxter.

"Sounds like a case with solid evidence. The name Julia Van Niekerk is a new alias to us. She has gone by Alana Weize, Roberta Canne and Jocelyn DuBris. She is suspected in four murders. Two in France, one in Norway and one in Singapore. None of these killings had anywhere the evidence you have found, nor a bona fide witness. She is a contract killer of the highest level. She can speak by our count some eight languages, changes her disguise frequently, and never stays long in the area of the hit. Your case also mentions the Woodruff Brothers. They have been on our radar for several years. We believe they are involved in major fraud, money laundering, drug smuggling and now murder. If you can fax me copies of your investigation to date, I believe Interpol and our resources could get you this perpetrator."

Red asks,

"Inspector, do you have any lead on this person? Without her confession and connection to Woodruff this case is going nowhere."

"Detective Blackman, I understand your dilemma, but this takes time and effort. With any kind of break plus your evidence we can apprehend her. Then her confession will solve your case and many others."

Both men looked at each other. They both knew it was a crap shoot, but they had no choice.

Joe spoke,

"Inspector, the copies of the case are on the way. Whatever you uncover right now is more than we have. Thank you for your assistance."

"Detectives my pleasure, when we get something positive, I will personally call you."

"Thank you and goodbye Inspector."

"Goodbye Detectives."

CHAPTER FORTY-FOUR

Cammaratta Case
1961

Sean was the first to see the Black Cadillac Brougham followed closely by a Black Ford Starliner. At the corner of Houston and Columbia they made a right turn and stopped in front of the closed gate. A man in a topcoat exited the Starliner and opened the gate. Both cars proceeded into the parking lot and parked in front of the open ramp door.

"K-23 to K-61 the in laws have arrived."

"K-61 Copy that. All units stay silent, await further orders."

The Starfire went down the ramp first. There they saw Waldo and the crew. The Ford's horn blared twice, and the big Cadillac came down the ramp. Four men exited the Ford, two others exited the front of the Cadillac. On the floor were five full duffle bags and a loose stack of cash totaling $5 Million. Closer to Waldo and the crew were three duffle bags and another pile of $5 Million. The back door of the Cadillac opened, and Waldo recognized Bobby Vitello. The other door opened and a man in a topcoat and sunglasses exited and started walking towards Waldo. He shook hands with Waldo, while Bobby checked the split.

Bobby gave the thumbs up, and two men picked up two duffle bags each, while another man bagged the $5 Million and picked the fifth duffle bag. They placed all the loot in the trunk of the Cadillac. With business concluded Bobby Vitello hugged Waldo and walked with the topcoat man back to the Cadillac.

The black ford Starfire started up and drove up the ramp and waited outside. Next the Cadillac started up and exited up the ramp. With the Ford behind them they exited the parking lot gate.

"K-23 toK-61 In laws on the move."

K-61 copy that. All units wait until we learn of movement."

Sean watched the Ford and Cadillac approach the Houston Street corner. He waited until he saw which direction on Houston they were heading. The Cadillac in the lead turned right followed by the Ford.

"K-23 to K-61 In laws heading toward East River Drive."

K-61 copies. K-61 to P-54 tells us if they go north or south on the East River Drive?"

"P-54 to K-61 Copy."

In less than a minute there was a reply.

"P-54 to K-61 to they are heading south."

"K-61 to Chief 22 they are all yours."

"Chief 22 to K-61 thank you."

"K-61 to K-23 Are you still waiting on the help?"

"K-23 to K-61 that's affirmative."

Meanwhile about a mile down on the East River Drive

"Chief 22 to Highway 3 and Highway 6 start your move.

"Highway 3 to Chief 22 ten-four".

"Highway 6 to Chief 22 ten-four."

"Chief 22 to ESU 68 and ESU 101 Proceed to your points."

"Chief 22 to P-54 take up position behind ESU-101."

Meanwhile Sean and Gus are now off the roof and parked on Columbia Street awaiting Waldo and crew.

"There they are, they are exiting the parking lot" said Gus.

"K-23 to K-61 The help is on the move."

"K-61 copy. Wait till they hit the corner."

"K-23 to K-61 they are in a Con Ed pickup and have made a right onto Houston."

"K-61 to all units set up forthwith. K-23 follow behind help, P-51, P-37 back K-23."

"K-61 to P-33 need you running west on East 2nd Street."

"K-61 to ESU-67 and ESU-72 Prepare for stop at Avenue A."

As the light at the corner of Avenue A and Houston turned red Waldo and crew were so happy they did not observe what was going on around them. If they had looked up, they would have seen the two ESU trucks blocking the intersection, nor did they see the police wielding shotguns shoot out the pickup's front tires. Waldo heard a knock on his window. He looked up and saw Gus aiming his revolver at him. Lorenzo said,

"Oh shit."

Sean had his .357 magnum revolver aimed at Lorenzo's head. Slowly looking around all they could see were cops with guns drawn. Hauled out of the pickup one by one, they were all placed on the roadway and cuffed. The duffles and a smaller bag were also placed on the roadway. Gus came over and knelt down near Waldo.

"Hi, Waldo, heard you were back."

On the East River Drive the stop had been made without a shot. Both cars were emptied, and everybody cuffed. The Cadillac trunk was opened and the five duffles and a single bag were removed. Chief Abrams pulled up to the scene and went over to Bobby Vitello.

"Do you know who you're fucking with?" asked a defiant Bobby.

"Yes, Bobby I do, just another low life thug in an expensive suit," said Abrams.

Abrams then went over to the man with the sunglasses. He reached over and took the sunglasses off of his face.

"Oh my, have we hit the jackpot. Guys let me introduce our prisoner, he is mob royalty.

Say hello to Mario Muscra, Joe Profaci's son-in-law."

Abrams saw how distressed Muscra was acting.

"Mario, Joe P is not going to be happy about losing all this loot, however you he'll write off. Have a great day Mario."

Abrams got on the radio.

"Chief 22 to K-61."

"K-61 to Chief 22 go ahead."

"Got them all Dougie. Righteous collar, see you at your squad."

"Thanks Charlie. K-61 over and out.

CHAPTER FORTY-FIVE

Conolly Case
1961

The celebration of the Cammarata bust went on for two days, then things quieted down for the Squad. Gus and Sean were heavily involved with the Queens DA in preparing the court case. Everything had to be gone over until the evidence shined.

Meanwhile, across the squad room Joe and Red glumly awaited a call from South Africa. It was crucial to the entire case. Red had gotten back his request for records for any stolen Ford Falcons, that came back negative. Lt. Simmons had not called, but Red was hoping this longshot came in. He looked at Joe and said,

"Joe, has this ever happened to you before trying to solve a case?"

"No kid, first time for everything. You know it's hard relying on someone you only talked to over the phone. If Mahlen cannot find her, the Woodruff's win."

"Well I hope he can find her. How about some lunch?"

"Sure, that dive around the corner will do" said Joe.

At lunch they barely spoke about the case. Instead, the talk was about baseball, the fire on the Staten Island Ferry, and Christine Keeler from the Profumo scandal in England. It felt good to get away from the work for even a few minutes. Upon their return to the squad room, they were greeted by Sgt. Crandall.

"You got a long-distance call from South Africa, here's the number to call."

Joe grabbed the piece of paper and looked at Red.

"Mahlan called."

He dialed the international operator and was told to hang up and remain by the phone. when it rang twice the call was connected. In a few minutes the phone rang twice, Joe picked it up.

"Detective Williams, this is Inspector Mahlan."

"Yes sir, we have been awaiting your call. Hope you have good news?"

"I do Detective, we have her in custody."

Joe smiled and gave the thumbs up to Red. Red jumped up high and pumped his arm upward.

"When did you get her?"

"Yesterday, she was caught at the airport leaving under an alias. She gave up without a fight and was brought to our office here in Johannesburg. We are now in our fifth hour of interview, our people say she is showing signs of weakening, but so far, no confession. I wish I could give you a more positive report, but this will take time. I will call you when we finish."

"Thank you, inspector, myself or Detective Blackman will be available at this phone twenty-four hours."

"Goodbye Detective Williams."

Red who had been listening on the extension placed the phone down and looked at Joe.

Red said,

The time now is 2PM, I'll take the first twelve, you relieve me at 2AM. Go home get some sleep, I'll wake you if he calls back."

"No argument from me, see you in the morning."

Joe slowly got up and walked out of the squad room. Meantime, Red busied himself with making the new entries into the crime book, updating the existing paperwork, getting all times and dates in order, putting the crime scenes in order. At about 6PM Sean came into the squad room. He saw Red standing at a file cabinet with his back toward him.

"Hey Red, how have you been?"

"Could be better when we close this case."

Then Red realized he and Sean had not spoken for a long time, he turned around and said,

"Great job on that bust. You and Gus hit the big one."

"Thanks. Learned a lot from it. What about your homicide?"

"Well, we have done everything possible, now we're waiting on Interpol in South Africa to close it for us. You feel useless like someone tied your hands behind your back."

"Look, all our hard work will be rewarded, you'll see."

"Sean, you sound and look like a veteran cop. Does making a super bust really change your looks?"

"Yes, I feel like John Wayne, Burt Lancaster and Roy Rogers rolled up into one."

They both laughed.

Sean then said,

"You think you know what to do because you were trained by the book, but when you work with a veteran partner like Gus it really opens your eyes to what is out there. All his years and the experience are what you have to learn. If you're going to succeed."

Red says,

"Same with Joe. I have been introduced to sources that are not mentioned anywhere in the book. Without his knowledge and expertise, we would never have gotten this far, from a dead guy in a Queens apartment to a suspect in South Africa. We're two lucky guys. If we're to become partners I'll break the cases, and you give the press statements with your John Wayne looks."

"No way Einstein, I'll do the interrogations, you collect the evidence."

They laughed and slapped their outstretched hands. Then Sean looked at Red and asked,

"What do you know about Peter Lugers, I promised my old man a steak, ever been there?"

"Once with my father, great steaks, reputation and expensive. When do you plan on going?

"Maybe in a few weeks?"

"You shouldn't go until they make you a Captain, then you can afford it."

Sean's face fell to the floor. Red watched and started laughing.

"Red you son of a bitch, I'm going to get you one day."

As both were laughing.

"Bring it on Beer, it will be fun."

The phone rang. Red hoped it was Mahlan, but it was Lt. Simmons.

"Detective Blackman I got a hit on some car rental information."

"Yes, go ahead."

"For those dates you gave me, I found a single Ford Falcon rental. Hertz has a lot on 10th Avenue, Manhattan. A white 1961 Ford Falcon was rented on those dates by a Lorraine Curtiss, 29 W.89th Street, Manhattan. NY Driver's License 899345186. Returned no damage."

"Thank you very much Lt."

"Are you new? There's more."

"Yes, I'm new this is my first investigation."

"Who's training you Brewer, Antaknockis, or Williams?"

"Joe Williams."

"He's one of the best they got over there. I told you I had more. Well Lorraine Curtiss at that address and drive license do not exist, you have a real ghost. Well, new Detective Blackman what are you going to do?"

Red thought, then said.

"The only thing I can do is to take a ride over to 10th Avenue and see if anybody at Hertz can give a description or verify her from the photo we have."

"Outstanding, you're going to be a Chief one day. Do me a favor, tell that lazy bum Crandall to call me, I'm not waiting for Christmas."

"Will do Lt. Simmons and thank you."

He hung up the phone and just shook his head.

CHAPTER FORTY-SIX

Conolly Case
1961

Her real name was Candace Vermaack, born April 8, 1930. Her parents were both professionals, father a maritime attorney and her mother an eye surgeon. She had an brother five years older. She was sent off to a Swiss boarding school at age ten, so she was safe during World War II. At the age of 20 she graduated the Sorbonne de Paris with high honors. Worked for several high-tech French companies then moved to Marseilles. She was beautiful, had money and could speak five languages. Roaming in the many social circles of Marseilles she partied nightly and became involved with a Corsican, Phillipe Saveriu. They fell in love and lived together on Saveriu's three estates and two yachts. Saveriu had made his wealth with the notorious Corsican Union and ran an exporting firm out of Marseille. Candace knew of his criminal history and accepted it. Saveriu smuggled heroin from Afghanistan and Turkey thru Marseille to the United States. In due time Candace became a 'mule' for him and a very good one. She expressed an interest to Saveriu in learning 'the business'. Soon she was introduced to the corrupt public officials and bankers, document forgers, ships captains, and hit men. Saveriu died in a motor vehicle accident, the now wealthy widow could have stayed in the safe luxurious life, but Candace developed a fascination with murder. She joined an Englishman named Jonathan Mills who taught her the art of assassination. She travelled the world with him and learned. The act of execution excited her, and the thought of taking another life was dormant in her psyche. Her first 'wet job' was in Canada. She posed as a nurse to gain entry to a critical care unit, where she injected the victim with a fatal overdose. She and Mills became a very highly paid team that was sought for their expertise and ease of operation. They had accumulated a vast wealth that afforded them a chalet in Switzerland and apartments in Paris, New York and Tokyo. Fate stepped in while they were on a job in Rome. Mills was caught, she escaped and sought safety in Corsica. She had been on her own since then acquiring more wealth and new properties. Her clients were amongst the world's richest and she was in demand for her services.

Now she sat dressed in orange coveralls and handcuffed to a steel table awaiting the questions from a Senior Interpol Agent.

"Ms. Vermaack, tells us about your trip to Norway in 1958."

"It was for pleasure."

"Do you remember the name Uwe Erickson? He was the president of Norge Hydro Electric."

"No, I do not recall that name."

"We believe you shot him point blank in the head, outside in his company parking lot on March 4, 1958."

"You accuse me of this. Do you have a photo of me?"

"July 21, 1957 Lisbon, Portugal you entered the country that morning and then you killed financier August Von Denza in his office. Who paid you for that assassination?"

"Let me see, I was in Paris that day for a meeting with the designers of Jean Bijou Couturiers, I was there the whole day buying dresses."

"Candace, tell us about Singapore November 8, 1958 and the accountant Sirhan Singh. How did you enter his home and kill him while he was sleeping?"

"I was in Singapore meeting with an artist to commission a painting for a client. Look, what is this all about? So far you have accused me of killing people I've never heard of. I told you I did not know those names and my being in those cities was mere coincidence. Prove to me I did what you said. Do you have a witness, a photo, anything? If you cannot show me, then let me go."

The interrogator took a new tact.

"Candace, who is Roland Woodruff?"

For the first time there was no fast comeback. It took her a few seconds to answer.

"Never heard of him."

"Do you know his twin Roland? He is in New York."

Again, she hesitated in her reply.

"Never heard of him either."

"That's odd. We have an eyewitness that puts you in Roland's New York office this year."

Her demeanor began to change, she did not reply.

"Do you know Gerard Conolly?"

"I guess you're going to say I murdered him."

"Yes Candace, we know you murdered Gerard Conolly and Phylis Taylor on orders and payment from the Woodruff brothers."

"Prove it!"

"Your hairs were found at the Conolly murder scene, your blood group was identified and matched, and trace elements of your expensive Marcel Vittan lipstick were uncovered."

"I do not use that brand."

"I beg to differ Candace. We have a witness at George Van Renna Co. who sold that brand to you. She identified you, even your Afrikaans accent. Now Candance I have a list of more evidence that will send you to the gallows on Robin Island. Now how far do you want me continue?"

With her head down, she began to shake. The interrogator gave her a bottle of water.

She finished drinking, looked up and said,

"What do you want to know?"

"Candace, it may worthwhile to you if you start with talking about the Woodruffs."

It was over. She admitted to the Conolly/Taylor murders as well as the other homicides. She was paid by the Woodruffs for the Singapore and New York murders $5 million. She implicated others for the Norway and Portugal assassinations. With a signed confession, Inspector Ben Mahlan made the call to the New York.

"Hello, Detective Williams, we have a signed confession. She implicated the Woodruffs for Conolly/Taylor and another murder in Singapore."

"Thank you very much Inspector Mahlan. We cannot thank you enough for closing this case.

Anytime you need help in New York City call me or Detective Blackman."

"You're welcome. I am faxing you the whole confession. I know you have some arrests to make. The best to you and Detective Blackman."

"Thanks, and goodbye Inspector".

It was about 8AM. Joe dialed Red's phone. A tired sounding voice answered.

"Get up Red. Mahlan called, she confessed, and we got the Woodruff's. Get dressed while I get an arrest warrant for Roland Woodruff drawn up and signed."

"Hey Joe, I'm going to call Sgt. Revelli to be there when we bust Roland."

"Good thinking kid, he helped us out and we need all the new friends and help the future can bring."

CHAPTER FORTY-SEVEN

Conolly Case
1961

The office was decorated for Christmas. In a few minutes the spirit of Christmas would have to take a step aside for the arm of Justice was about to come down.

Roland Woodruff's secretary Joyce tried to stop the three men from entering her boss's office. When the arrest warrants were shown she stopped in her tracks. The door was shut but Joe just opened it. Roland Woodruff looked up and said,

"I do not have an appointment with you Detective, see my secretary."

"Roland this is my partner Detective Blackman and Detective Sergeant Revelli from the Hoboken Police Department. They are here to serve you with arrest warrants and inviting you to our place of business."

"Roland Woodruff you are under arrest for the murder of Gerard Conolly" said Red.

"Roland Woodruff you are under arrest for the murder of Phylis Taylor" said Revelli.

"Put the cuffs on him Red."

Woodruff was flustered and resisted, but Red quickly forced him to comply. He yelled,

"Joyce call my attorney!"

"Oh, by the way, with your arrest I will get your client listing without any legal mumbo jumbo."

All eyes were on him as he was paraded out into the main office. Joe saw Marci and gave her a quick smile, she smiled back. After this is over, I'm going to marry that girl, thought Joe.

CHAPTER FORTY-EIGHT

102ND Squad
1961

About three days after the arrest of Roland Woodruff, Interpol agents and British Police arrested Ronald Woodruff at Heathrow Airport bound for Cuba. The Conolly case was over and now the prosecutions began. Sgt. Crandall came up to both Red and Sean and told them Lou wants to see them. Inside his office they found Gus and Joe seated and a man in a suit standing.

"This is Lt. Fusco from Internal Affairs" said Lou.

"Detectives Blackman and Feeney, you are both under investigation for neglect and exceeding your authority. Detective Feeney did you fail to mark into evidence the bolt cutters found on Thaddeus Zoldy?

"I thought I marked everything found. Can I see the casebook with the evidence listing?"

"No, you may not."

Detective Blackman we have a complaint from one Gloria Edmonds of George Renna Company that you made a disparaging remark about her breasts. We will investigate these complaints and in the meantime you will surrender your weapons and badges to your Lieutenant now."

Stunned they both placed their badges and weapons on Lou's desk. There was silence in the room.

Lou, "You both know as your commanding officer I can send you both back to the TPF for these infractions".

Is there anything else Lt. Fusco?" asked Lou.

"Yes, tell these two gullible greenhorns Gotcha!"

Gus and Joe let out a laugh, and Lou was almost crying.

"Son of a bitch, we were played" said Red.

Fusco came forward and offered his hand to both Red and Sean.

"Detective Inspector John Rivera, Queens Homicide, pleasure to meet you both.

Sean now smiling said,

"You really had me going."

Rivera departed the office. Lou shoved their badges and weapons towards Sean and Red.

"Take these backs and listen carefully because I rarely say what I am going to say. Guys like you two are rare in this business. They come around maybe every ten years. We are usually left with a heavy and difficult task of trying to make a good detective. Red and Sean, you have far exceeded our initial observations. Now I will add you both as a team to this squad. I hereby unleash you upon the citizenry of New York City, may God have mercy on their souls.":

Joe looked at Red,

"Red, I have had partners who never knew what to do. You took this on like a duck to water. You listened and went beyond what I asked. You and your partner will be good together, the chemistry is there. The best of luck to you."

Gus got up,

"Sean, we have seen them come and go thru here, but you have been the exception. Your alert, quick on your feet and your mind. It was my pleasure to have guided you. Best of luck."

Lou adds,

"Ok enough of these platitudes. Sgt. Crandall has you both at the far corner desk with one phone. Now get to work you're dismissed."

CHAPTER FORTY-NINE

Detective Partners
1962

The new young team started making a name for themselves. They started to close cases at a nice rate. Their success was due to the lessons Sean learned from Gus, have a working street network. Sean and Red each month contributed out of pocket to their 'snitch fund'. The fund proved valuable for information was gold. Their reputation started the night they went into Pepe's Bodega at Forbel and Stanley Street for some sandwiches. Both of them were enamored with the Cuban sandwiches made by the owners, the Ramos family. They entered, said hello to Mrs. Ramos at the register and went to the back sandwich counter. As Sean and Red were ordering their sandwiches from Pepe Ramos, two-armed street thugs walked in. Brandishing a cheap Saturday Night Special and a double-barreled shotgun, they held Mrs. Ramos by her hair and demanded the register money. With only some $123.00 in the register, the pistol bearing thug hit Mrs. Ramos across the face. Hearing her scream Red went low and moved up the left aisle, while Sean moved low up the right aisle. The thug was about to hit her again, when Sean yelled,

"Police! Drop your weapons now!"

The guy with the shotgun turned to fire at Sean, Red put a .357 magnum bullet between his nose and top lip. He went down fast. The other bandit now with two cop guns on him grabbed Mrs. Ramos and placed his gun to her head. He yelled,

"I'll kill her you mother fuckers! I'll kill her!"

Red sighted his weapon and said to Sean,

"This is definitely a Routine Six situation."

"I agree," said Sean.

"OK, I'll count to six."

Sean replied,

"Go ahead start counting."

The thug was wide eyed and looking at Red as he started to count.

"One, two, thr...."

Sean's shot took off the right side of his head. Mrs. Ramos was unhurt, and she hurried to the back screaming towards her husband.

Red got on the phone and called it in requesting an ambulance and morgue wagon. There was a flurry of people coming down from upstairs. The Ramos children, all six of them were relieved to see their parents. Responding units enveloped the street. The partners waited for Sgt. Crandall to show and the department shooting team. Crandall arrived first and came over. He asked if each of them was alright. Then he wanted the particulars. When they finished, he said.

"You both did the right thing, I'm okay with this. Tell the same to the shooting team."

As they waited, Red was approached by the oldest son Ruben. He was about twenty and built like a tank.

"My name is Ruben and I want to thank you for saving our mother. I don't know what we would have done if they killed her."

Red put his hand on the man's shoulder.

"She's a brave lady. Your family are good people, and good people are to be protected. We just did our job."

"Well thank you both."

Sean asked,

"Did you ever see these guys before in here?"

He looked at the one who had the gun and said,

"He was in here yesterday; they call him Roach."

"Thanks, we'll look him up. Ruben, we came here for your great sandwiches. Mr. Ramos was almost finished with them, any chance of us getting them so we can eat?"

Ruben look at them and asked,

"Why do you call my father Mr. Ramos his name is Pepe."

"I know that, but out of respect we rather call him Mr. Ramos."

"You're the first gringos to show respect most of the cops that come in here call us 'spics'"

Red replied,

"I'm sorry for that but my partner and I are not like that."

Ruben went to the back and in a few minutes was back with the wrapped sandwiches.

"Here, no charge."

Red and Sean took the sandwiches and went over to the register. Ruben came over and said,

"On the house."

"No Ruben, every week we come in here and pay $6 a sandwich. Here's $12 take it or we leave the sandwiches here and find another bodega."

Ruben took the money and smiled.

"Detectives, in our culture those who save a life, the family is indebted to them. Please, my parents would say the same thing."

Sean and Red handed him their cards.

"You keep your eyes and ears open, then gives us a call. We may come to you for information, that is how the Ramos family can pay us back."

Ruben extended his hand to both; they firmly shook hands and then the shooting team showed up to ask their questions.

The first stage of their 'Street Telegraph" started with Pepe's Bodega and was soon joined by Caterina's Bodega ten blocks away whose new owner was Ruben Ramos.

Sean had learned from the best, Gus Antiknockis. You needed street people be it victims, perps you caught, drug users, ex-cons or the homeless. They had to be treated alike, dangle the reward get the right information. A good detective had to have a good network, and that network extended in other ways. If a snitch needed a safe place to stay or hide from pursuers you had at least five safe houses to stash them in with no questions asked. If they needed food you could tell them where to go and give your name, and if they needed clothing that also would be taken care of. All this worked and soon Red and Sean had a working intelligence gathering capability on the street. The Street Telegraph was humming all about the young cops who treated you with respect, so they were given a name appropriate for the street, Bagels and Beer. One day an informant of theirs called Criss Cross walked in wanted to speak to Bagels, he had some information. Sgt. Crandall had no idea who he was talking about, but he took the guy's name and told the visitor he would let Bagels know. When the change of shift occurred most of the detectives in the squad were present, so Crandall asked if anybody had a snitch named Criss Cross. Red said he did.

Crandall said,

"Then you must be Bagels. What's your partners name, Cream Cheese?"

"No Sarge, it's Beer" said Sean.

The squad room erupted in laughter, and from that day on the name for the young duo stuck.

CHAPTER FIFTY

Homicide Case
1962

The back area of Aqueduct Racetrack is where the horses are stabled. It is also where those that train the horses work and live. A trainer is usually assigned a section of stables to work from. Here he has his own workforce of grooms, hot walkers, exercise riders, stable muckers, office personnel, assistant trainers, cooks and dishwashers. Nearby the stables are the bunkhouses where those that care for and feed the horses can sleep and be readily available. The evening meal had concluded and most of the stable hands would watch TV, play cards, dominos, or just lay in their bunks. The horses were for the most part fed and watered and would soon lay down on clean hay. It was about 10:30PM when there were noises coming from outside the bunkhouse. Several of the hands got up and went outside and found hot walker Johnny Rushmore fist fighting with groom Clevis Hill. Rushmore was already bloodied, but he kept moving towards Hill. As Rushmore moved to launch a right, Hill countered and hit him squarely on the jaw knocking him unconscious. All believed the fight had ended. Hill came back into the bunkhouse and floppded on his bunk, stomach down.

Ten minutes later a revived Rushmore entered holding a four-inch knife, he stabbed the sleeping Hill eleven times in the back. Hill somehow rose from his bunk coming up with his five-inch knife and thrust it directly into Rushmore's heart killing him instantly. When the responding motor patrol arrived, they found Rushmore with the knife still in his heart, and Hill barely breathing but alive, against a wall bleeding profusely. They called for an ambulance and their Sergeant. He arrived in two minutes, saw the scene and requested a Detective team from the 102nd.

In the squad room Red was clearing up paperwork, and Sean was going over evidence from a burglary.

The time was about 11:10PM when Red received the call. He took the information and grabbed his jacket and the keys to their car.

"Let's go Sean, we got a body."

"Where?"

"Stable area of Aqueduct Racetrack."

The car that was assigned to them was a clunker. A 1961 Dodge Savoy with some 115,000 miles.

You had to stand on the gas pedal to get it up to 60 mph, and the ride was bumpy due to old and never replaced shocks. When they finally arrived at the bunkhouse, they found the body of Johnny Rushmore awaiting the Medical Examiner. The assailant was on his way to the Emergency Room at Jamaica

Hospital. Red spoke to the responding patrol officers and their Sergeant. He was shown the bunk where the assailant was stabbed, and the blood trail when he got up. The assailant was named Clevis Hill, employed by Valley Ridge Stables as a groom. He was stabbed eleven times in the back by one Johnny Rushmore, a hot walker employed by the same stable. Red asked if they found the knife Rushmore used.

The Sergeant pointed to a knife laying on the floor. Red pulled out an evidence envelope and with a pair of tweezers he picked up the knife and sealed it in the envelope. He looked back at the bunk and saw a piece of paper protruding from under the mattress. It contained dates and numbers. He placed that in an evidence envelope.

Sean was standing over the body of Johnny Rushmore. A knife was protruding from his chest area, the victim also had a bloody mouth. Sean asked the Sergeant if there were witnesses. He stated they had six people who saw the fist fight outside, and five people who saw Rushmore stabbing Hill in his bunk.

The Medical Examiner arrived. He introduced himself as Dr. Alvin Stoddard. Putting on his rubber gloves he started to examine the body.

"Detectives, know anything about this bloody mouth?"

"Yes, there was a fist fight outside, and he was knocked unconscious for about ten minutes"

He then touched the imbedded knife, then he pulled it out. Red was there with an open envelope and the doctor placed it inside. Reaching into his bag he removed a needle like instrument and stuck it into the body. He took the temperature of the liver and stated,

"Death was about an hour ago give or take a few minutes. Death was instantaneous with the knife thru the heart. I'll do an autopsy and if something unusual shows up I'll call you. Detectives can I remove the body?"

"Yes, you can," said Sean.

The ME gave the signal and two men came in with a black body bag and a stretcher.

"Thanks Doc," said Red.

"Good meeting you, see you around."

Sean and Red stayed around for about fifteen when one of the patrolmen came over to say the Head Trainer of the stable had arrived.

Both Sean and Red identified themselves. He was a tall man, wearing a cowboy hat. He said his name was Tommy McArthur and he was the head trainer and owner of Valley Ridge Stables, Paris, Kentucky.

Red asked,

"Mr. McArthur, we understood both the victim and the assailant are your employees. How long were they employed by this stable?"

"Johnny had been with me for six years. Clevis has been here for some 16 years."

"Did you know of any trouble between them?"

"No."

"What was Rushmore's job?"

"He was a hot walker. When the horse finishes a workout, he continues walking him till they cool down. "What was Hill's job?"

"My main groom. He took care of my top horses. Fed them, watered them, made them pretty for the race."

Sean asked.

"How many horses do you have in this stable?"

"I brought up twenty-five from Kentucky for this meet. I have another fifteen stabled in Pimlico."

"You own all those horses?"

"Oh God no. I train for the owners of the horses. These twenty-five I have up here represented 14 different owners."

"Is your stable considered big by track standards?"

"No, I'm small compared to those who I call the Three Jays. Jacobs, Jones, and Jerkens. They have big stables and the winners to prove it."

"Well thank you Mr. McArthur, if we have any more questions, we know where to find you."

"Detectives, I'll be pulling up my tent here in 10 days. Racing is like the circus, we continually move. I'll be up in Saratoga all next month."

"Best of luck to you."

"Thanks."

Red and Sean got back to their car. Sean looked at Red.

"Red, what do you know about horse racing?"

"I know if I bet on a horse and the track is muddy, and that horse comes in last, he's a mudda fucka."

"You're insane" said Sean laughing. "No really, we both know nothing about this sport. My Uncle Brendan is a gambling degenerate. He bets on horses and loses every time I find that dumb, but there's more to this we have to know."

"Well after we talk to Hill at the hospital, I'll ask around the squad, maybe somebody knows somebody."

CHAPTER FIFTY-ONE

Rushmore Case
1962

Jamaica Hospital was a city hospital. It was busy, loud, and in need of an overhaul from the basement up. Clevis Hill had been in surgery over five hours. They somehow kept him alive and were able to sew the pieces together. He was now in intensive care hooked up to a breathing machine and poked with at least five lines of medicine dripping into his body. He would be unable to talk until he could come off the breathing machine. The attending physician demanded of Red that the handcuffs be removed that secured Hill's wrist to the bed. Red stated it was NYPD standard procedure that a prisoner be bound this way, and the uniformed officer outside his room would remain at all times. The doctor reluctantly understood and began to calm down, and Sean asked,

"Doctor, when will be able to speak to him?"

"The next two days are critical. If he makes it through, he should be able to speak."

"Thank you, Doctor, we will be checking in."

As they left, they both knew that this case was open and shut. There would be an indictment and maybe a trial. If it went to trial the defense would insist Hill acted in self-defense and acquit him of murdering Johnny Rushmore. What they had to learn was why Rushmore initiated the attack? So right now, they had to learn a lot more about Johnny Rushmore. They would run a criminal and financial check on Valley

Ridge Stables and Tommy McArthur. Heading back to the squad Red said to Sean,

"I'll ask Joe Williams if he knows anybody in the racing industry then maybe we'll understand what we're getting into."

Twenty minutes later they entered the !02nd Squad room. It was busy with Detectives taking statements, working on paperwork, leaving for a new case. Red saw his mentor Joe Williams.

"Hey Joe, Sean and I grabbed a homicide at Aqueduct Racetrack and need some direction."

"What do you need Bagels?"

"We need someone who knows all about thorobred horse racing?"

Joe looked around the room, saw Sgt. Crandall and he motioned him over.

"What do you need Joe?"

"Not me, but Bagels here needs someone with knowledge of the sport of kings. Can you direct him?"

Crandall grabbed a piece of paper and pencil and wrote an address.

"You and Beer be at this address at 10 o'clock tomorrow morning. I tell him to expect you."

"Thanks, Sarge."

CHAPTER FIFTY-TWO

Rushmore Case
1962

The address was 890 Melville Road, Farmingdale, NY. They entered the gate of a very large fenced in area. They could see horses standing in a field and a circular training track. At the end of the long driveway was a building whose sign said Long Island Equine Institute. They enter and tell the receptionist they are expected. She takes their names, then buzzes a number.

"Gentlemen, please be seated, he'll be here in a few minutes."

Soon a man in late thirties wearing an open neck shirt and blue jeans arrives.

"Which one is Beer?"

Sean raises his hand.

Then he looks at Red and says,

"You're Bagels."

He shakes their hands and say his name,

"I'm Tom Crandall, head veterinarian of this place. Come on in, we'll have coffee in my office."

They arrive at his office and are seated. On the rear credenza is a photo of their host with three uniformed NYPD officers, and one of them is their Sergeant Crandall.

"Are you related to our Sergeant?"

"Yep, he's my oldest brother."

He grabs the photo and points to the older man. This was my father's retirement photo, he retired as a Deputy Inspector, Manhattan North."

"Who's the Captain?"

"My second brother Ted, He runs the 28th Precinct in Manhattan.

"We did not know the Sarge came from a family of cops," said Sean.

"Well big brother Byron has always been quiet. He and Ted have bumped heads since they were kids, but you ask Ted who is the best cop in the family he'll always say Byron."

"So, what happened to you? asked Red.

"I never wanted it, animals were my passion, so I followed my dream. Graduated Cornell Veterinary School, went into the Army continued there with animals then came out and became the head Vet for the New York Racing Association. Did that for ten years, then the owners built this place for research and equine development. That's my story. Now I understand you want to know all about horse racing."

Red started,

"Doctor Crandall, we grabbed a homicide case at Aqueduct the other night. The guy who did the killing will probably walk because it was self-defense. The victim initiated the attack and both of us are wondering, were there outside forces at work? We know the street, but the racetrack does have a different reality?"

Just then a female in a lab coat enters and places paperwork on his desk. Sean just stares at her; she is drop dead gorgeous. Blond hair and blue eyes, pert nose and great legs.

"Bridget these are Detectives Blackman and Feeney, they work with Byron."

"How nice to meet you. How is my biggest brother, that big teddy bear?"

"He's your brother? Everyone here related?" asked Sean.

"Yes, this is Dr. Bridget Crandall, DVM my partner and baby sister."

said Dr. Tom.

"Now you know the dark secret of the Crandall family, not everyone is a cop." she said.

They all laughed.

"You tell Sgt. Teddy Bear I love him, and for him to call me."

"We will," said Red.

As she left the office, Sean could not get her out of his head.

Dr. Tom looked at Sean and said,

"Sorry Detective Feeney, she is already engaged to a Naval Officer they are getting married when he comes off his cruise."

"The best of luck to them" was all he could say.

"Now to the subject you came to hear. On January 1st of every year, all horses have a birthday. Does not matter if it was born in September 1961 on January 1st, 1962 you are a one-year-old yearling. Blood lines are very important. If its mother (broodmare) was a champion or has lines to great champions and she mates with its father (stallion) who was a champion and has great blood lines than maybe the yearling will be a champion of like caliber. Here is the biggest 'If '. People will spend millions of dollars on these untried and untested horses based on the maternal and paternal blood lines, but the odds of this horse being a champion is extremely high. What if the yearling does not take to training?

What if the yearling has lacks speed or endurance? What if the yearling is prone to injury because of weak bone structure? This is why taking ownership of a horse is one big gamble. There are more failures in this industry than successes. It is not an investment for just anyone. In my opinion you have to have a lot of money, and the ability to not dwell upon your investment wondering why your horse does not win, or you will go insane. The trainer and his stable are very important here. Here your horse will be taken. care of and hopefully will learn how to race. The best trainers know if a horse can race, and the honest ones will be truthful with the owners as to the future of their horse."

Red asks,

"Can I ask you about a trainer who came up in our investigation?"

"Sure, if I know him, I'll tell you straight."

'Tommy McArthur?"

"Cowboy Tom. Good trainer been at this for years. Worked as an assistant to the great Sylvester Veitch. He knows horses, but he is also good at knowing his owners. He is one of those guys who will tell you straight if you're wasting your time or to have patience and see how the horse develops.. Has a medium to large stable based in Kentucky. Last year he was the best trainer at Saratoga with some thirty wins. Liked by all, never heard anything negative."

"Thank you, that gives us a better perspective."

"Getting back to racing. If a horse wins and brings in money, then the ownership is happy but bringing in money depends on the type of race they win. On any given race day, you may have one high cash race, and your horse can win a lot of these type races, however the Grade One and Grade Two races are what define the champions. These races are the big money races and carry with them the prestige of winning a race that is considered a true test. A male who wins a lot of money during its racing career is worth more to owner if he goes to stud. Here other owners pay for their female horse to copulate with the champion male. These stud fees can run from $5000 up to over $150,000. Once again, the offspring are a big question mark and gamble. Now let's talk about some of the other people involved other than the owner and trainer. The jockey is an independent contractor. The trainer will pick the jockey. He advises him how he wants him to ride the horse, when to step on the pedal and what other horse to stay away from. If the jockey places he gets a share of the money pool after the owner and trainer. Yes, there have been jockeys who are crooked. They have ridden favorites to dead last against the trainers advise or used illegal items to stimulate the horse. They eventually are caught and banished from the sport. An honest rider will make a lot money if they are good. Look at the program and who is riding in every race, you keep seeing the names Arcaro, Ycaza, Hartack, and Shoemaker. The jockeys have agents who let the trainers know their client is available. They get a percentage of what the jockey wins per race.

"Is there cheating in racing?" asked Sean

"Unfortunately, yes. Look, there is always a group that cannot be trusted, and racing has and had some of these. People have rigged a raced. They want a longshot to win and make a lot of money. In order to do this, you would have to involve others, namely the jocks riding the favorites. Drugs are another factor. They may stimulate a horse to run faster than ever before, but they may endanger the horse's health. Testing the horse's urine is the best way of determining illegal drug dosage. Another way of making money on horses illegally is setting a barn on fire, killing the horses, and collecting the insurance.

This happens over and over in this business and it is just another illegal and immoral method."

"Well thank you for your time Dr. Crandall, you have been a great help. I think we have a better idea on what we are investigating." said Red.

"Tell me Doctor, who might we talk to who has an ear to everything happening in the backstretch?" asked Sean.

"Only one person, Red the Baker."

CHAPTER FIFTY-THREE

Rushmore Case
1962

Returning to the Squad, Red immediately went up to Sergeant Crandall and gave him the message from his baby sister. A rare thing happened. Crandall smiled and thanked Red.

Back at their desks, the phone rang, and it was Jamaica Hospital. Clevis Hill was up and awake, he could answer questions. Off to the hospital in their "speedster", they arrived in fifteen minutes. Hill was awake eyes opened and still cuffed to the bed. They identified themselves and started the questioning.

"Mr. Hill, what caused the fight between you and Johnny Rushmore?" asked Red.

Hill took a few minutes to answer then he said,

"Bobby's Girl"

"Who is Bobby's Girl, a horse or a woman."

"She's the best filly to come along in a long time for Valley Ridge. Johnny wanted me to fix a race for him, but I don't do that. He kept on nagging me to do it, so I pushed him away, then he swung at me.

I swung once and knocked him out. Thought that was over and went to sleep on my bunk, then he is stabbing me in the back. I always keep my knife handy and came up and I stabbed once, then he was dead."

"Any idea why Johnny wanted you to fix the race?" asked Sean.

"Johnny always found trouble. He gambled and he owed money to some bad people."

Red asked,

"Did you ever hear who these bad people were?"

'The track has a lot of people that work there. There are some that are like leaches once they get hold of you, they don't let go. Johnny had them on his back, that's all I know."

"Do you know how they were going to make the filly lose the race?" asked Red.

"Probably slip something into her pre-race food, but I watch everything that goes into bucket."

"Do you think Rushmore ever tried this before?"

"Not a Valley Ridge, maybe some other place, but not at Valley Ridge."

"Do you know where Rushmore came from before he was hired at Valley Ridge?"

"None of the big tracks. He said he worked tracks in Arkansas and Ohio."

Red asked,

"We found this under your bunk mattress. Is this your writing? What does it mean?"

Hill looked surprised.

"Yeah this my writing and it's my record for all my horses. I kept it to make sure they were healthy and ready to race."

"How did you determine that?" asked Sean.

"The horse tells you by their eyes, the flair of their nostrils, their coat and belly. How they eat is important. Do they eat all their food or only eat a little? A horse can tell you if he or she is ready to race.

"Did you ever find a horse not ready to race?"

"Twice this season, the same horse. I thought he needed a few more days, so did Mr. Tommy but the owner wanted him run. He raced and lost bad."

"How bad?" asked Red.

"Came in seventh out of eight horses."

"What was the name of that horse?"

"McIntosh, like the apple. Great bloodline, his mama was Pas de Nom, daddy was Northern Dancer.

First time he goes off at 4 to 1 and loses to four bad longshots. I get him back in the stable and his eyes were cloudy."

"So, you think he was tampered with prior to the race?" asked Sean.

"Strange things sometimes happen in racing."

"Mr. Hill, who owns McIntosh?"

"A big fat Russian guy from Brooklyn, can't say his first name, but his last name is Malkin."

Sean spoke,

"Thank you, Mr. Hill for your time, you have been most truthful and cooperative. I am going to leave a card for a good attorney I know. Call him and let him plead your case."

"Thanks Detective, appreciate that."

Red motioned for the officer outside to come in.

"Officer, this prisoner presents no security problem, please remove his cuffs, but remain outside."

Clevis Hill smiled and gave a thumbs up to Red as they left his room.

CHAPTER FIFTY-FOUR

Rushmore Case
1962

At 8AM Red and Sean had gained access to the Aqueduct backstretch. They watched with amazement the business generated by this one food truck. Long before starting at 3AM the stables came awake. Another day of training would begin and the regimen of feeding and grooming, exercising and walking would begin all over again for the equine population. Assistant Trainers holding stopwatches, mounted exercise riders galloping on the training track, horses finishing their workout and being hot walked, and even the delivery of fresh hay to the stables announced that the day has started. And in the center of all this activity was the high-side food truck run by Red the Baker. It seemed like every second someone came up to the van to get a donut, hot coffee, a soda or a sandwich. Behind the counter was an older man with dark red hair tinged with white and an assistant dispensing the food.

"Man does a lot a business" said Sean.

"Look around, see any competition?" replied Red.

"You're right, he's the only vendor."

"And that makes him the best source of information at this racetrack."

At about 10AM they observed the owner and assistant preparing to close. Getting out of their car they walked over and identified themselves. Red the Baker was a short man with glasses and a large nose.

He also possessed a pair of arms that were loaded with muscle. Red moved and walked like a prizefighter in the ring, and Detective Blackman recognized that.

"How can I help you?" he asked.

"Doctor Crandall told us to see you" said Sean.

"Oh, what a great guy. How is he?"

"He's fine, sends his regards."

"Well if he sent you, I will try and help you out. I'm going to guess, you're here about Johnny Rushmore, right?"

"Yes, we caught that case and we need to know what you might have heard?" said Red.

Red looked at the Detective.

"Do they call you Red, Detective Blackman?"

"Yes, they do."

"We share the same nickname. What's your first name if I may ask?" said the Baker.

"Morris. Morris Blackman from Bay Ridge."

"My name is Louis Schwartz, Avenue T, and I've been a baker for many years, and I'm Jewish. You know I never met a Jewish detective; it is nice to know the Police Department is progressing. Always seemed to be a private Irish club. Oh, forgive me Detective Feeney, no offense intended."

"None taken, Mr. Schwartz"

"Ok, fire away boys."

"Did you know the victim, Johnny Rushmore?" asked Red.

"Yeah, I did. Didn't think much of him. He got himself involved in trouble; seems trouble was always around him."

"What kind of trouble?"

"He owed a shylock a lot of money, and he was trying to outhustle everyone he came in contact with."

"Got a name for the shylock?" asked Sean.

"Johnny Rosario. Used to be a stable hand, got caught dealing drugs, banned for life. Now he has a crew out of Queens and swims these waters like a shark."

"So, what was your take on his murder Red"

"Johnny need to throw a race. He thought Clevis would help him, but Clevis would never do that, he's a good man."

Red looked at Sean and nodded his head, indicating this verified what Hill said in his hospital room.

"You know Clevis Hill?"

"For over twenty-years, good and honest man."

"Red, do you know if Rosario has hooks into anyone around here?"

"Probably a quarter of the stable hands they always need money."

"This Rosario, is he an independent or does he work for the mob?"

"Which mob are you talking about?"

"What other mob is there but the Mafia." said Red.

"Let me let you in on a secret, and make sure you tell everyone in the NYPD. The other mob is in Brighton Beach and it's the Russians. Russian Jews that make Murder Incorporated, Bugsy, Lepke and Lansky look like kindergartners. Rosario is connected to them. My guess is they needed a non-Russian face."

Sean looked at Red and knew it was time to leave. He said,

"Red, you have been very helpful. Appreciate you giving us your time. Thank you.

"You'er both welcome."

He shook hands and looked at Red Blackman.

"Be careful boychik, these Russians are crazy"

Red smiled and returned to the car. In the car he said to Sean,

"We got a case of self-defense which means Hill will go free. Rushmore is dead and cannot tell us about Rosario. We can't go after Rosario, so this case is technically over, unless something out the blue happens."

Sean said,

"I heard of those names from the thirties and forties. Those were tough killers, but from what the Baker said these Russians are crazy and vicious. I have a feeling they may be the ones that come out of the blue, God help us."

CHAPTER FIFTY-FIVE

Steven Witt
1962

9003 East Shore Road, Great Neck, NY was 25 acres on the Long Island Sound. Considered an estate it belonged to the Witt family since 1887. Their family fortune was based on gold and silver mining fortunes before the turn of the century. During the 1900's with a lot of money to invest the Witt founding fathers backed Henry Ford and Walter Chrysler in their beginning ventures. Soon they were buying ships and sailing the world with the manufactured goods of America in exchange for the natural resources and minerals of the world. Airlines, pharmaceuticals and oil exploration companies were purchased and again proved profitable. Harvey Bedford Witt, the present scion, had married Boston brahman money and with it came an electronics company called Raytheon. Forbes had named him the fourth richest billionaire in America. Every Sunday edition of the New York Times had Mr. and Mrs. H. Witt posing at some high society activity or a charity ball. There were three Witt children, two of whom graduated with Ivy League high honors, while the last child was asked to leave Princeton. Steven Witt, the former Princeton attendee, always wanted to be like his father, extremely wealthy. He wanted the wealth but did not want to put in the time and effort that was needed to keep it. Harvey would not accept his son was a lost cause. He was given a house on 5th Avenue, a red Ferrari, and the title of Director-Witt Corporation. Steven partied hard at the best clubs and nightspots, always seen with at least two beautiful women on his arms. His father required him to work at different Witt companies and subsidiaries with the hope he might learn something and take an interest in the family business. However, Steven had an addiction, a gambling problem. Sports bets on a single game for $100,000 were frequent and weekly. Las Vegas trips were numerous and costly it seemed he never won, but he kept on betting. While Steven was working at a Witt company his betting with his own personal bookmaker Jack Berg of the Sands Hotel and Casino was burning up the phone lines. Steven owed Jack Berg $3.5 million and Jack now wanted his money. Steven was paid a courtesy visit to determine when Jack Berg was going to receive his money. Steven took this first visit as an insult and told the envoy to tell Berg to fuck off. When Jack got Steven's answer, he asked for a meeting with one of the Sands owners. The owner listened as Jack told him who Steven was and the amount of debt he had accumulated. At the end of the meeting Jack Berg was made whole with a $3.5 million check, and the assumption of Steven's debt was taken over by the Sands. In the underworld, situations involving people like Steven Witt can prove to be profitable. The word went out from the Sands, they had a fish on the hook, that showed potential of providing more than just a meal. In the underworld this was code for you pay us our fee and this person is yours to exploit. Within a week those that were interested responded. The starting price for the Sands was $5 million. The winning bid came from New York at $6.7million. Steven Witt and his debt now belonged to Sandy Malkin aka Yevgeny Malkovich, leader of the Brighton Beach Russian mob. Unbeknownst to Steven Witt, he was the match that lit the fire that would soon be coming of the blue.

It was beautiful fall day in the city, and Steven, after a night of drinking and drugs, woke up with a headache. Getting dressed quickly he decided to go down to the local coffee shop and get his wake-up fix. Turning the corner off a 5th onto 62nd Street, he failed to notice the black van slowly rolling up to him. The side door opened, and two men jumped out and grabbed him forcing him into the van. Inside he was bound, gagged and a hood placed over his head. Steven thought he was being kidnapped as the ride seemed eternal. About 40 minutes later the van stopped and he was forced to walk aided by two persons on either side of him. Walking downstairs he heard doors open and was forced to seat in a chair.

The restraints were all removed and then the hood was taken off. He was looking at a male dressed in a black suit with a gold tie. The man was smoking a cigarette and offered one to Steven. Steven took the cigarette and placed it on his lips, a hand appeared from his right side with a lighter. Steven inhaled and looked at the man and said,

"If this is a kidnapping? we can get this over quickly."

"No Steven, not a kidnapping, but an opportunity for you to stay alive."

"What do you mean by that?" asked Steven.

"Very simple. You give us information about certain Witt Corporation facilities and operations, and you remain alive. You refuse I will take off your left ear."

"Whoa wait a second not so fast. Who the hell are you?"

"You remember Jack Berg? You owed him $3.5 million, well we paid him off for you, and now you owe us $6.7 million. You will give us inside information about the following Witt locations; Dynex Pharmaceuticals in Union, NJ, and VBS Television in Dover. DE. or we kill you piece by piece."

It was a rare choice by Steven, he chose to be bold and heroic and replied,

"Fuck you!"

All the man in the suit did was nod and two pairs of hands grabbed Steven and forced his head down onto the table with his left ear exposed up. Steven saw a box cutter appear in a hand and he felt it near his ear lobe. He screamed out,

"Ok, ok I'll help you, don't cut off my ear please!"

The box cutter went away, and Steven was placed back in his chair. The man in the chair said,

"Good choice, Steven. Here is my card and phone number. We will start first with Dynex. We need to know when the

Centro is being shipped. We need the time and dates, the locations, and the security involved. You got a week to get this information to me, or you will be back here with your head on this table. Do you understand me?"

"Yes, I do."

"Steven, the boys are going to hood you up and return you to 5th Avenue and 62nd St. Make sure you get some coffee. Call me when you have everything I asked for, until then goodbye."

When the van arrived at 5th and 62nd, Steven was let out. He decided to return to his home.

In his hand was the business card the man in the suit handed him. It simply said,

Mr. John Rosario

212-929-3816

CHAPTER FIFTY-SIX

Café Odessa, Brighton Beach
1962

Steven Witt had delivered. Johnny Rosario was now able to plan the heist of six truckloads of the drug Centro. Today he was meeting with the boss, Sandy Malkin at one of his businesses. In the back of the café Malkin was waiting and anxious to hear the plan. As Johnny entered Malkin rose up gave him kisses on both cheeks.

"Well Johnny, tell me what you got."

"Boss, we will follow the six trucks from the plant in Union. We know that three are scheduled to arrive in Robbinsville at a customer's warehouse. From Union to Robbinsville is some 55 miles and the obvious route is the NJ Turnpike, which is not a good place to stop them. So, we will do it in the customer's parking lot. Trucks are scheduled to arrive after midnight. We will take out the gate guard and knock, out the outside cameras. There are no security people inside the warehouse. When the Dynex trailers arrive, we check them in and tell them to drop the trailers outside the warehouse loading dock. As the three tractor drivers leave, our three tractors staged across the street move in, hook up and bring the three trailers to the East New York warehouse."

"Good, I like what I am hearing so far, continue."

"The fourth trailer is scheduled for a customer in Montreal. We follow this one in a tractor with a 3 man crew, and a car. They wait until the driver takes a leak or stops for a coffee. My crew in thirty seconds can start up the tractor, we then hookup our tractor and head back to East New York. The car driver and an extra man drive the original tractor some ten miles up the road and leave it. Then the car heads back to East New York. The fifth trailer is scheduled for Eastern Indiana. We learned the name of the trucking company hired for this load. The owner of this company is in our pocket, so he is making sure his cousin stops at Phillipsburg, NJ and walks away from it. We will be following with 2 guys in a car. They watch the cousin leave, then will take the tractor and trailer back to East New York. Now the sixth and final trailer is scheduled for Virginia Beach. This one we are hiring a Cuban crew from Miami. They will not stop until they reach the Port of Miami where the trailer will be placed on a ship for Genoa, Italy. Our Italian broker guarantees us that trailer load will return us some $22 million."

"Got one question Johnny. The Cubans taking the entire tractor/trailer to Miami, can't they be stopped once the cops get the word?"

"Yeah, I asked them about that. They will pull into any shopping center that has a paint store. If the tractor is white, it becomes blue. Any signage on the trailer they will paint over.

All of this done in the parking lot with long brushes. They can be out of there in less than fifteen minutes, because they let the paint dry while they are moving down the highway."

Malkin started laughing.

"OK Johnny, good job. Let me know when everything is safe and sound in East New York. When is this going off?"

"We have already started Boss; all our crews are now setting up. I'll be calling you in the morning."

"Come Johnny, a vodka toast."

CHAPTER FIFTY-SEVEN

Four Days after Dynex Heist
1962

The theft of six trailer loads of prescription pharmaceuticals hit like a bomb. Federal authorities gathered in Washington DC and decided to form Task Forces in the major cities. NYPD was asked to contribute their personnel. Some twenty detectives were required, so Lou offered up Bagels and Beer. Initial meetings were at the New York City Office of the FBI. Red and Sean listened as experts from the DEA explained Centro was a pain reliever for persons undergoing radiation treatments for cancer. The chemical makeup was such that when cut and the chemical Ammonium Caltrate was added, an addictive powder was produced that was twice as powerful as heroin. The prediction was street use would hit an all-time high. All officers would be deputized as temporary US Marshalls, thus giving them Federal arrest powers. The New York Task Force would work out of Floyd Bennet Field at the former US Navy Air Station. All members would report to a DEA Chief Inspector on Mondays and Thursdays every week.

Red and Sean started working the street. Any info on Centro was worth a $50 bill. The entire department was on alert. It did not take long. Red got a call from a Narcotics officer in Brooklyn South. His street informants and undercovers were hearing that two dealers at the corners of Cropsey Avenue and 15th, and at Bath and 17th were drumming up business. They were described as two male blacks, one wearing a blue Brooklyn Dodger cap, the other wearing a Jets Cap and Jets shirt number 78. Red told the officer they would make a buy within a few hours using one of his street sources because they needed to determine if this was coming from the NJ heist. The officer agreed and told Red to let him know the results. Red got hold of Sean and they were off for the Boulevard. Sean saw him first.

"Red, look over at the bakery, isn't that 'Sticky'?"

"Sure is, we'll meet in the alley."

They drove slowly, flashed their lights and Red rolled down the passenger window. Sticky saw them and started walking toward the alley. They drove around the block and entered the alley, Sticky was behind a wall, they stopped, and he jump in the backseat.

"What do you guys want? I got no warrants."

"We're not here to roust you Sticky, want to earn fifty bucks?" said Red.

"Hell yeah, what do I have to do?"

"Go to Brooklyn and see if you can score some Centro."

"I ain't got no money."

"This is a city sponsored purchase, we provide the money, you purchase the product."

"Ok, and then I get my fifty bucks?"

"Yes, Sticky you'll get your $50, you know we don't lie." said Sean.

"Yeah, I know you're two good guys."

They parked on Cropsey Avenue. Sticky got and out Red gave him three twenty-dollar bills.

When he reached the corner of 15th Street, he saw the guy with the Dodger cap. Small conversation followed with the dealer looking in all directions, then there was an exchange. A few minutes later Sticky was back in the car.

"What did you get?" asked Sean

"Two tabs of Centro, $10 a piece, gave him $20."

He handed them over to Red, who placed them in an evidence envelope.

"What were his prices?"

"Eight tabs for $75, just took the two."

"Good job Sticky, now let's try the other guy."

They went over to Bath Avenue, and then turned on 17th. At the corner was a guy dressed in Jets regalia with the number 78.

Parking above the dealer Sticky got out. Red gave him $35 in cash. In a few minutes he handed over eight tabs to Red."

"He took $75 for those." said Sticky.

Red turned around and handed Sticky a $50 bill. Sticky smiled.

"Ok we're heading back to Queens, that ok with you Sticky?"

"Just drop me off at 86th Street got to eat something."

They dropped off Sticky and drove to Floyd Bennett Field. They turned over the purchases to the DEA for testing. They would now have to wait for the testing results.

Patrick Burke was a corporate vice president of Security. He was now outside the office of Harvey Witt for a scheduled private meeting. Since the Dynex heist he had slept only once. The information he had would not be taken happily. The door opened and Witt's secretary motioned him inside. As Burke entered, she departed. Burke took a seat reaching into his briefcase he pulled out a folder. Harvey Witt looked at Burke and said,

"How bad?"

"$36 million bad. Six trailers fully loaded. Only found two of the tractors. Everything just disappeared. I've been in touch with the FBI. The DEA has started a regional task force that includes all Federal and local law enforcement. I have made myself available if anything surfaces."

"What do you think Patrick?" asked Witt.

"Someone on our inside gave out some valuable information. This was so right on the mark with four different hijack locations."

"I want them caught. Do you have any idea who it might be?"

"Not right now Mr. Witt, but I will start surveilling our entry and egress systems, and any off-hour entries."

CHAPTER FIFTY-EIGHT

VBS Television Company, Dover, Delaware
1962

It was the long Labor Day weekend. The roads of the industrial park were empty of all traffic except for a large black Lincoln Continental with NY Plates. Johnny Rosario sat in the back seat with a handheld radio. It was time to begin.

"Ok squirrel start."

The technician opened the telephone box and searched the wire grid. He found the building alarm circuit and activated an alarm. It took fifteen minutes for the first Dover PD car to arrive. Another ten minutes to check the doors and gates and he left the property. Johnny waited about a half an hour before he radioed the tech to do it again. Again, another fifteen-minute wait then the PD arrival, followed by ten-minute check and then they left. He waited one hour and again repeated the alarm activation. However, the response this time took some thirty-five minutes. With the police leaving again after checking the property, Johnny now radioed,

"Acrobat start."

On the western side of the Shipping building were two ladders that went straight up to the roof. Twelve figures, all in black clothing, climbed up to the top of the roof. One rope was thrown down to a support person on the ground, who attached a gas driven rotary saw. In a few minutes a large hole was cut into the roof, and three rope lines were anchored. The twelve-person team now slid down the ropes onto the main warehouse floor. Twelve forklift trucks were started and proceeded over to the more expensive color television sets made by VBS. Pallets containing twenty sets were moved and staged in front of the outgoing shipping doors. Soon, twelve loading dock doors had some thirty pallets ready for loading. The inside leader radioed to Rosario,

"Acrobat waiting."

Rosario spoke into his radio.

"Transport go."

Within a minute, twelve white tractors and trailers came into the Industrial Park and the main shipping gate was opened. Each truck with its trailer door open backed into the shipping dock. The truck leader radioed Rosario,

"Back in complete."

Rosario spoke into his radio,

"Squirrel loop it."

The alarm technician now attached three alligator clips to the three outgoing alarm terminals.

To the central alarm station everything at VBS was alarmed, when in fact the connections were creating a continuous signal of protection. The technician then radioed,

"Squirrel complete."

Rosario spoke once,

"Raise them up."

Twelve overhead doors raised up and the first pallets were loaded. The entire loading operation took less than twenty-five minutes. The trucks pulled away from the dock some ten feet. Then each of the forklift drivers jumped off the dock and locked the trailer doors shut and got into the passenger seat of each tractor. The twelve tractor trailers then drove up US. Route 13 North to the Delaware Memorial Bridge and connected with the NJ Turnpike. Crossing the George Washington Bridge, they threaded their way to the warehouse at Wortman and Essex in East New York. The sign on the building said East Brooklyn Distribution Associates owned by a shell company named Brighton Partners. The job netted Malkin some $7 million and made him very happy.

Patrick Burke was not very happy. This last theft was very costly, and he and his staff went full steam looking inward. The one thing in common between Dynex and VBS was someone had gained access to shipping information and building plans. This did shrink the employee population from twenty thousand to some four thousand. Each and every one of these four thousand was investigated. They were able to eliminate about seventeen hundred persons whose jobs did not put them contact with anything related to shipping information or physical plant layout. Another two hundred persons were eliminated due to retirements, workman's compensation and long-term disability. Now down to twenty-one hundred persons, the process started with who had access to shipping information and who used building plans. This eliminated fifteen hundred, leaving a final group of six hundred. Now Burke's people started matching the jobs to the access. Who received on time shipping plans? Who needed to see the blueprints for the buildings? Witt Company Engineering Department maintained all building plans at a rented building in Manhattan. A check with the head of Engineering showed that building plans were handled by request. A request had to be filled out, and a copy of the building plans were then company mailed to the requestor. The check of requests for the VBS building plans was initiated, and a list was forwarded to Burke's desk. In the case of Dynex, an investigation into who was on the list to receive shipping information. That list was also sent to Burke. When Burke went over the listings, he found a single name that was both common to the Dynex and VBS investigations, Steven Witt. He made the call.

"We found the insider." said Burke.

"Who?" asked Harvey Witt.

"Your son Steven."

"Jesus Christ, bring him to the house tonight Patrick."

"Yes Sir."

CHAPTER FIFTY-NINE

102nd Squad
1962

Red got the call from the DEA chief at Floyd Bennett, the tablets that Sticky had purchased were Centro, and had come from the Dynex Pharma heist. Red gave him the information on the two dealers and their location. He then made good his word and called the Narcotics Officer who gave him the initial information. Meanwhile Sean received call from their old classmate from the Academy, William Washington.

"Where are you working? asked Sean.

"Still in the 1-0-1 working Narcotics. How's Red?"

"He's still crazy, and I have to watch over him."

They both laughed.

"Heard you two are becoming urban legends, even have bona fide street names. So, your Beer and he is Bagels?"

"Yeah, it really stuck, sometimes I forget that my name is Feeney."

Washington laughed again, then said,

"Sean, I called because I saw your bulletin on the Centro heist. I arrested a user for some heavy possession, and he wants to deal. When I asked what he was going to trade, he tells me knows who was in on the Centro heist. Do you two want to talk to him?"

"Hell yeah. When can we see him?"

"He's here in holding, won't be shipped out for another three hours."

'We are on our way."

"Bagels, we got a guy who knows something about the Centro heist. He's sitting in the 1-0-1, Bill Washington grabbed him for possession."

"Our Bill Washington?"

"Same one."

"Wow, old times."

It only took them about 10 minutes to get to the neighboring precinct. Seeing Washington, they all embraced and chatted. In the interrogation room, Washington brought in his prisoner and cuffed him to the table.

"Guys, this is Ronnie Lewis he would like to cooperate."

"You said you know who was in on the Centro heist?"

Looking at the ceiling he started to hum a tune. Red slammed his hand on the table and Lewis jumped out of his seat.

Sean and Washington smiled at each other.

"Hey asshole! I didn't come to hear you hum a tune, I'm here for information, now talk or we don't deal!"

Having got his attention, Lewis started to talk.

"I drove a car to Phillipsburg, NJ. My passenger was a truck driver. We were told to go to a lot off Route 22, and the keys would be in the truck. I followed him back to East New York then dropped the truck, trailer and car at a warehouse."

"Where was the warehouse, what street?"

"Wortman Street off of Essex. Hey, I want to know what your deal is before I say anymore?"

Red looked at Washington.

"We'll reduce your charge to possession under two ounces, less than a year Rikers versus the five years your facing now."

"Ok, what else you want to know." said Ronnie.

"Where did you follow the truck from."

"We knew the truck number. We waited at the Route 22 West exit in Union, saw the truck and followed him to the address in Phillipsburg. The truck and trailer pulled into the address and we watched the driver get out and walk away. Stayed there and watched the truck for one hour, saw no cops around, my passenger got out, keys were left in the ignition. He drove to East New York, I followed in the car."

"What was the driver's name?"

"Never asked him, and he never asked me for my name."

"How much did you get paid?"

"I got $3000 bucks for five hours work." Lewis said smiling.

"How did you get this driving job? asked Sean.

"A guy I knew from prison gave me a call. Wanted to know if I wanted to make some quick money."

"What was his name?" asked Red.

Lewis again looking up at the ceiling. Red looked at him and said to Washington,

"The deal is off, send him up for five. You're useless to me Ronnie!"

Now Ronnie dropped his act, this cop was serious.

"Hold on, I'll tell you. Name is Barney Vickers, white guy lives in Queens, that's all I know.

"Ronnie, good choice." said Sean.

They exited the room with Washington and thanked him for his help. Now they had a decent lead.

CHAPTER SIXTY

Witt Estate, Great Neck, NY
1962

Steven Witt stood before his father. Patrick Burke was seated off to the side. Harvey Witt wanted an answer.

"Steven, we have the proof that you sold out our company. You have caused us a great loss in revenues, and I want to know why?"

He began to shake, his eyes misted, and he looked at his father.

"They own me dad. They would have cut off my ear if I had not cooperated."

"Who are they?"

"I don't know, but they bought my marker from my bookie, and now I owe more than before."

"How much did you owe your bookie?"

"$3.5 Million."

Harvey Witt was astounded. He had no idea his son had gambled.

"Steven, how much do you owe these other guys?" asked Patrick.

"$6.7 Million."

Burke interrupted,

"Mr. Witt. Steven's marker to his bookie was paid by another entity. Then this entity put up for bid Steven's potential future worth. That was sold to a third entity for the $6.7 Million. Now this entity is getting back from Steven his knowledge of the corporation so they can perpetuate these crimes. Steven will never be free of them."

Harvey sat down to think. There was silence in the room.

"Steven, sit down and please do not talk."

Steven sat down immediately.

"Patrick, you have been working with the FBI, would they be able to figure this out like you did?"

"When we met, it was agreed that if our internal investigations found anything linking to the crimes, that information would have to come from me. As far as they know I have yet to find anything."

"Alright, this is how it is going to play out. Steven you're going away for a very long time. You will not have any communication with me, the family, or the company, until these people are no longer interested in you. Patrick will set you up in a country where you will live. You will take on a new name

and try to keep a low profile. Money will be set up in an account for you via monthly transfers. You are not to gamble on anything, for if you do there will be no inheritance for you. Do you understand?"

"Yes, I understand."

"Patrick, get him out of my sight and get him packing as soon as possible."

"Dad, I'm so sorry....."

"Too late for that Steven, now leave."

Two days later with a new passport and name Steven walked into his small chalet nestled between the Alps in Zug, Switzerland.

Patrick Burke said,

"Your new name is Alois Kelner. You were born in Zurich and you have no family. Every month your father will send you money. Here is your Swiss driving license. There is a car in the garage, here's the keys. This is your life from now on Steven. You will have no contact with your father or the rest of the family. No gambling they are watching and waiting. I have to catch the flight back to New York."

"Thank you, Patrick." said Steven.

The next day Alois Kelner drove into Zug to look around and buy the necessities. English was easy and he had taken courses in German, so he could get by. People were friendly, the mountains were majestic, yet his previous lifestyle was out of the question. He returned to his house and found a tourist guide to Zug. On page six he smiled. Daddy must have forgotten to check out Zug. This place was the home to ten casinos. Steven had given his word and he was warned not to gamble again. The odds were against him if he started gambling, but the old Steven always went against the odds. Anyway, he said to himself, I have a new name nobody will know.

CHAPTER SIXTY-ONE

Fresh Meadows, Queens
1962

Barney Vickers was at home, he even answered the door. Red and Sean identified themselves and said they wanted to talk him outside. Vickers of medium height and weight got his jacket on and went outside. On his driveway they talked. Red began,

"Barney, I'm going to cut to the chase here. We know you were involved in the drug heist in Union, we have witnesses. Here's my offer to you. Tell me what I need to know, and we will walk away and never come back here. Refuse, and we all go back to the precinct and you will rot in prison. This offer ends in one minute."

Sean looked at his watch and said,

"One minute starts now."

"Hold on, hold on, if I talk, they will kill me. All I did was drive a big Lincoln around Brooklyn that night that is all I did."

"35 seconds left."

"Wait a second will you? Look I may have seen something, but I had no idea what they were doing!"

"Bullshit, 15 seconds."

Vickers stood there shaking, his mind running like a roller coaster.

"Times up, Barney Vickers you're under."

"Okay, I'll talk but you have promise once I tell you what you want to know, you two will never come back."

"We said it, we meant it. Now how many drivers did you recruit for that job?"

"I got them eight drivers."

"How much did you get for that?" asked Red.

"I got $10,000 for that night, plus I drove around the guy who ran the show."

"Where in Brooklyn did you drive?"

"All over, Prospect Park, Bay Ridge, Canarsie, Coney Island."

"Who was the guy you were driving around?

"Some mafia guy."

"Hey dummy, he pays you ten large and you don't know his name, what's his name?" asked Sean.

Vickers was hesitant, he was scared.

Red said,

'Enough, Barney you won't talk, deals is off the table, cuff him Sean."

"Wait, his name was Johnnie Rosario."

Red and Sean knew that name from the Rushmore murder, now it surfaced again.

"How did Rosario know to call you?" asked Red.

"He knew I could get drivers fast and no questions asked."

"You said you drove all around Brooklyn, did you drive over to East New York?"

"Yeah, I did, how did you know?"

"What's the name of the warehouse where all trucks with Centro ended up? You know the warehouse at Wortman and Essex." asked Sean.

"Jesus, you guys know everything. The sign on the place said East New York Distribution Associates."

Red asked,

"When you were driving Rosario around, who else was in the car?"

"There was a gun carrying bodyguard up front with me, and Rosario had a guy he talked to the whole trip."

"Try to remember what they said to each other." said Red.

"When we got to Coney Island the guy in back wanted to stop at Nathans Rosario said no.

In Bay Ridge Rosario said he could never find a good Italian restaurant."

Sean asked,

"Come on, did he say anything about the heist?

Vickers thought awhile then replied,

"When we got to the warehouse, he said something like, Steven was right, there were six trucks."

"Do you know who this Steven is?" asked Red.

"No never heard that name before."

They were finished with Vickers; he had given them good information. It was time to leave.

"Barney, here's my card. You call us if you remember anything else or if Rosario calls you again." said Sean.

Vickers just nodded as he watched the two detectives leave.

CHAPTER SIXTY-TWO

102nd Squad
1962

They both went to see Lou and told him about what they learned from Barney Vickers. The warehouse in East New York and its ownership had to be checked out. Lou was insistent that they keep the DEA abreast of this new Information. The Rosario name was reported, and they asked Lou what he knew of the Russian mob in Brighton.

"To be honest with you both, I know very little. We have heard that they are organized within the community but little else so far it seems contained by the local precinct. Let's get Sgt. Crandall and Williams and Antaknockis in here"

Soon, all were gathered in Lou's office.

"Bagels and Beer got a case where the Russian Mob in Brighton Beach came up. I know very little about them. What about you guys, heard anything?"

Gus tells them,

"I got some family in Sheepshead Bay, saw them a couple of weeks ago. My cousin Nick told me that the Russians are buying up property all around, cash up front and price is no problem."

Sgt. Crandall joined in,

"Funny you're asking about this. My baby brother Tom told me the New York Racing Association banned an owner from racing his horses. Its unusual an owner gets banned. Seems they did some due diligence and found out he had a criminal record in Russia. Name was Sandy Malkin and he lives in Brighton Beach."

"That name surfaced in our Aqueduct stabbing case, he was a horse owner trying to throw races." said Red.

"And this guy named Rosario was owed money by our vic who was trying to fix a race for persons unknown at the time." said Sean.

"Joe, you got a friend in the Organized Crime section FBI New York?" asked Lou.

"Bernie Rodriquez, good guy. I'll give him a call."

"And find out about this East Brooklyn Distribution Associates, who owns it, and who owns the building. Okay everybody get back to work."

As they both got back to their desks, the phone rang.

"Detective Blackman, 102nd Squad."

"Detective, this is Red the Baker."

"Yes Red, what can I do for you?"

"Well, I may be doing something for you. Come over now to the backstretch, I'll wait."

"We're leaving now."

It took them about thirty minutes with traffic, but Red was still there inside his truck.

He saw them and motioned them over to the back of his truck and opened the doors,

"Want to buy a color TV, they are cheap."

"How much?" asked Sean.

"$300 less than what they're asking at Macy's. The reason I called, is the guy I bought it from owes Johnny Rosario money. This TV has got to be hot."

"We'll just copy down the serial number if it is hot. Can you give us a name?"

"His name is Larry Chalmers, assistant trainer for Hirsch Jacobs."

Sean said,

"Thanks Red, we'll check him out."

"Enjoy the television Red." said Red.

"Thanks, Red."

Back at the Squad, Sean made a call to Department Intelligence. They maintained a record of stolen merchandise city, statewide, and national. Sean spoke to an officer and gave him the serial number, make and model of the TV set. He was on the phone for maybe five minutes, when the officer came back on the line,

"Detective Feeney, that set was stolen from the manufacturer in Dover, Delaware less than a month ago. Loss of $7 Million in merchandise reported by owner VBS."

"MO of the theft?"

"Done over the Labor Day weekend. Entry thru the roof. Twelve shipping doors found wide open and gate locks cut off."

"Thank you." said Sean.

Sean told Red of the burglary in Dover, Delaware and the TV serial number they had copied down matched one of the sets stolen.

Red had a hunch. He called his father who was a long-time investor in the stock market.

"Hello Dad, need a favor."

"Sure, what do you need Morris?"

"Ever hear of a manufacturer of televisions called VBS?"

"Yes, they make color televisions, very good ones I am told."

"I need to know who owns them. Is it a single person or are they part of a group of companies?

"Let me call my broker, he'll know in a minute. Can I call you back?"

"Thanks Dad, call me at the Squad."

Sean knew something was up in Red's mind for he always stared at something and was silent.

Joe Williams came over and sat down with the two.

"I just got off the phone with Bernie Rodriquez, my buddy at the FBI. They have been on this Centro heist since the start. It seems that the owner of Dynex Pharma was not very helpful in providing internal information, so the FBI went digging on their own. They got a hit in Las Vegas off a mob informant. Seems a son of the owner of Dynex was into the mob for millions of gambling debt. His marker was paid and auctioned off and sold to the highest bidder. The high bidder was a Russian in Brooklyn named Malkin. Goes by the American name of Sandy Malkin, real name Yeugeny Malikovich. Born in Odessa, Russia 1920. Top assistant to Russian mob boss Semion Moglievich. Came over to US with family in 1953. Owns several businesses and properties in Brighton Beach, Brooklyn, including East New York Distribution Associates. To date no arrests, however he is a person of interest in several investigations of money laundering, loan sharking and gasoline tax schemes."

Red was quiet and he stared straight ahead, then he asked,

"Joe, what was the name of the owner's son?"

"Steven Witt."

"Steven said there were six trucks. That's what Vickers heard Rosario say when he was driving him around the night of the Dynex heist." Said Red.

"Looks like you got some more evidence guys." said Joe.

The phone rang, Red picked it up.

"Detective Blackman 102nd Squad."

"Morris, my broker found that information. VBS is a subsidiary of the Witt Group of companies owned by one man, Harvey Witt."

"Thanks Dad, you're the best, and kiss Mom and Grandpa for me."

"I will, but stop by, we all miss you."

"When I finish this case, you'll see me thanks Dad.

He looked a Sean, smiled and said,

"Feeney, me boy let's check out that warehouse I got a feeling it's chock full of Centro and TV sets."

CHAPTER SIXTY-THREE

Café Odessa
1962

Johnny Rosario was escorted to the back-dining room. Two large armed men were guarding the door. Johnny was let in, then the door closed behind him. Seated at a table with a bottle of Vodka and two glasses sat Sandy Malkin.

"Johnny my good friend, please sit"

Rosario smiled and took a seat. Malkin poured some Vodka into the glass, then poured one for himself.

He lifted his glass and said,

"To the future, may it be just as profitable as the past."

Rosario touched his glass to Malkin's, smiled and took a sip.

"Now tell me, what are you and the "Golden Son" working on next?"

"Mr. Malkin, we can't seem to find him."

"What do you mean you cannot find him? He was your responsibility. We agreed in the beginning we would squeeze every drop of information out of him. Without him, you have no value to me Johnny."

"I know I got all my people looking everywhere for him. From here to California the word is out for him, but nothing has surfaced."

"There are other ways to get a bear out of its cave. I suggest you use them, and right away before it is too late for you."

Rosario stood up.

"I will take care of this immediately Mr. Malkin."

Malkin waved his glass,

"Good night Johnny."

Thanksgiving 1962 was over. People were back to their jobs, pupils returned to school. The cab from the New Haven Railroad Station came to a halt outside the gates of the Gunnery. Eighteen-year old Harvey Spencer Witt, son of Harvey's middle son Keith was returning to the halls of this famous boarding school.

He was a junior and a starting forward on the basketball team with an eye on attending Princeton.

As the cab pulled away, he gathered up his luggage when a van pulled up, the driver's window came down and a voice asked him for directions. As the young man got closer to the driver, the side door of the van slid open and he was grabbed and thrown inside the van. His hands were tied behind his back, and a hood placed over his head. A voice said,

"There is a gun aimed at you, do not give us any trouble and you will be alright."

The van then started back west toward New York and Brooklyn.

Two hours later Harvey Witt took the call.

"We got your grandson. He wants to talk to you."

"Grandpa, I'm okay. I don't know where I am. Why did they take me?"

Harvey knew young Harvey's voice, he cringed. The next voice he heard was Rosario's.

"Mr. Witt, the boy is alright as long as you cooperate."

"What do you want from me?"

"Steven Witt's location. Once we have Steven, we free the boy. Give me your answer in one hour."

Then the line went dead. Witt dialed Burke and told him to come to the house. Twenty minutes later Patrick Burke was at the house.

"Patrick, young Harvey was taken, they said they will kill him unless I tell them to where Steven is."

"You asked me to protect Steven and make sure he is safe. I did that and have protected him to a point. My sources in Zug report Steven is gambling again and maintaining a high profile, just what we told him not to do. Do not forget Harvey, he caused you a lot of serious damage. The life and future of your grandson is more important."

Thirty minutes the phone rang. Witt picked it up. He listened then told Rosario Steven's location in Zug.

"When we secure Steven, your grandson will be released."

Then he hung up.

CHAPTER SIXTY-FOUR

Outside the East New York Distribution Associates Warehouse
1962

Their unmarked car had a heater that whispered. They had been watching the warehouse for any activity, but so far only a Chinese food delivery. Red said to Sean,

"Do you see any outside security on this place? If they have what we think is in there, there should be an army of armed muscle watching this place?"

"Maybe that is the way Malkin operates by keeping the overhead down."

"Could be" as Red laughed.

Another sixty minutes went by when they saw a straight body truck pull up. The driver jumped out and went into the building.

"Sean, start it up I need to see if there is anyone else in that cab."

Sean slowly drove past the truck, then Red jumped out. On the sidewalk he walked back down toward the truck. Seeing nobody he went to the rear of the truck withdrew his gun and smashed the right rear brake light. Sean came around and parked, Red got in.

"What did you see?"

"No one was in the cab, so I broke the rear brake light."

"Now why did you do that?" asked Sean.

"So, we can have a reason to stop him. Whoever said we had to be nice?"

In a few minutes the driver came out and drove the truck over to a loading dock. The door opened and he was taking on a load. After some twenty minutes they watched the driver start up and leave the dock.

He headed in the direction of Interboro Parkway heading north.

"Stay on him Sean, I'm calling in the cavalry.

"K-6 to Central. "

"Go ahead K-6. "

"Need investigative stop on Interboro heading north white straight body GM NY plate 567WE9 broken tail-light, any Highway Unit."

"Highway 22 responding one minute out."

"K6 to Highway 22 10-4."

The Highway unit was upon them, then passed. Lights and siren on he pulled the truck over. Sean pulled over in back of the Highway unit. They stayed in the car as the two highway officers questioned the driver. Five minutes went by, when one of the officers came back to their car.

"He's nervous. He produced a regular driver's license in the name of Alexi Rogovoff, Brighton Beach, he has no chauffer's license which he needs to drive that truck. So far, we have two violations,"

"What is he hauling?" asked Red.

"Cardboard."

"Jesus, Red he doesn't have what we're looking for." said Sean.

"What do you want me to do Detectives?" asked the Highway Officer.

Red went silent, Sean knew the wheels and gears were running he motioned to the highway cop to wait.

"Have him open the back, then bring him back to the front. Write him up, Sean and I will check out that cardboard."

The door was opened, and soon Sean and Red were climbing into the back of the truck.

"What are we looking for Red?"

Red reached into a pile of cardboard and pulled out two crushed boxes. He said to Sean,

"Read the labels on these boxes."

Sean's eyes went wide as he read,

"Centro 50mg tablets. Batch 4589RE21 Date of manufacture 5/22/62. Dynex Pharma".

They went deeper into the pile. Sean pulled out a flattened larger box. He read the writing on the box.

"VBS Color Television 18 inch. Serial #D835667TD98".

"Twenty to one these numbers will match the stolen load in both heists, Sean get one more TV box and one more Centro box. Make sure they have the labels on the box." said Red.

With the evidence in hand, they motioned to the highway officers to finish the stop. Returning to the Squad, they made the calls that verified the evidence.

Meanwhile;

At Idlewild Airport, two large men were escorting Alois Kelner off of a Swiss Air Flight. A large black Lincoln was waiting for them outside the terminal. The rear door was opened for Kelner and as he got in a smiling Johnny Rosario said,

"Hi Steven."

Some fifteen minutes from Idlewild. Again he was placed in a van with a hood over his head. Two men were in the back with him. The trip was maybe thirty-five minutes. The van stopped, the door was swung open. He was guided out and his hood taken off. The brightness took a while to wear off, then he knew where he was. Harvey Spencer Witt was in Great Neck and he started walking down his grandfather's long driveway toward the big house.

CHAPTER SIXTY-FIVE

102nd Squad
1962

They met with Lou and showed him the empty boxes and that the labels matched what was stolen in both heists.

"Good work. Now we have cause for a search warrant. I need you to take that extra set of boxes you grabbed from the truck over to the DEA at Floyd Bennet. Tell him to call me forthwith, and we will set up a joint raid on the warehouse. What else do you have to do on this case?" said the Lou.

Red

"Joe's friend at the FBI said they believe the son of Harvey Witt was the insider for the Dynex heist. A Las Vegas informant reported the son had a gambling problem and owed a few million to a Las Vegas bookie at the Sands Hotel. Sands paid the bookie then auctioned off the debt to all comers. Winning bid came from Brighton Beach, Russian mafia boss Sandy Malkin, who happens to be Johnny Rosario's employer. They own Steven Witt, who had knowledge of Witt Corporation operations. We interviewed the recruiter of drivers for Johnny

Rosario, who stated he heard Rosario say, "Steven was right, there were six trucks". Steven Witt is the person whose debt Malkin owns and is the youngest son of Harvey Witt."

Red stopped and smiled. The Lou looked at him and said,

"So, where do these TV boxes come in?"

"I was hoping you would ask Lou. VBS the TV manufacturer in Delaware that got hit is a subsidiary of the Witt Corporation."

"Jesus, this Steven gave them up too." said the Lou.

"He sure did, and I think big daddy knows that, and has made his son disappear for the time being."

"Give those boxes for the DEA to Rossi and Sinclair tell them what I said. I want you two to visit Mr. Witt right now and get him to tell you where this Steven happens to be, or we will be charging him as an accessory.

They both left the Squad to find Harvey Witt.

Two hours later at the Witt Corporate Headquarters, Harvey was in a meeting with corporate marketing when his secretary appeared and whispered in his ear.

A rather disturbed Witt exited and saw Red and Sean standing in the hallway.

"Detectives, I'm in an important meeting, what is this about?"

"We want to talk about Steven." said Sean bluntly.

Witt was kind of stunned, he ushered them into his office and shut the door. Regaining his composure, he said,

"My son is out of the country. What is this about?"

Red explained,

'We have reason to believe your son Steven was the insider giving information to a group of criminals who perpetrated the thefts at Dynex and VBS. We have reason to believe you helped Steven in his flight which makes you an accessory to these thefts and obstructing our investigation. So, Mr. Witt be truthful now, so we can save your son and capture these people."

Witt sat down behind his desk and bowed his head. After several seconds he looked up and said,

"They kidnapped my grandson and were going to kill him, I had to tell them where Steven was."

"Where is your grandson now?" asked Sean.

"He's safe and back at his private school."

Red asked,

"When your grandson was returned that meant they had Steven, am I correct?"

"Yes, they have him."

"Mr. Witt, where else in your other operations was Steven trained? asked Red.

Witt had to think for a while, then replied

"Wyoming at our natural gas fields, oil fields in Venezuela, and our diamond operations in the Netherlands."

"When Steven is no longer of value to them, he will be killed. Do you want to see that happen Mr. Witt?"

"Oh God no."

"Then be truthful with us and help us try to determine what part of your corporation will Steven tell them to hit next."

He looked at Red and said,

"If I could, I would tell you right now, but we have some 150 subsidiary companies. I could not even tell you where to begin."

"Mr. Witt, please be available, we may learn something from our other sources, and we will need your cooperation at that time."

"I understand Detective."

Meanwhile

Johnny Rosario's home in Douglaston, Queens.

Steven Witt was locked in a small basement room, guarded by two armed Rosario associates.

The door opened and in walked a smiling Johnny Rosario.

"Welcome home Steven. You've been a bad boy, leaving me just when we were making money.

"Start talking or it is going to get bloody."

Steven knew he had to give him some good information, but at the moment all he could think of was his father's house.

"There is a lot of jewelry in my father's home."

"How much?" asked Rosario.

"Maybe $4 million worth."

"No, not worth it. Think of something else Steven, or I am going to pry out your left eye."

"Wait!"

Rosario motioned to his two men and drew a knife out his pocket and expertly flicked it open.

"Hold his fuckin head down say goodbye to your eye Steven!"

His head was grabbed and forced upward toward Rosario. Steven started screaming as he saw the point of the knife get closer to his eye. Then he remembered. He remembered Amsterdam.

"Stop, stop I will tell you."

Rosario withdrew the knife and motioned his men to release Steven.

"This better be good or I will cut off your dick."

"They have a diamond house in Amsterdam. It is called Baron Incorporated. Every week a shipment arrives at Idlewild and is picked up by armed courier. The courier brings it to the Baron offices on 47th Street."

"How much?"

"Smallest shipment I ever saw was $85 million."

"When and where does it arrive at Idlewild?"

"From private flight from Amsterdam arrives Idlewild at 6AM every Wednesday. Tail number on plane is PH1007. Plane pulls up to TWA Cargo gate and the diamonds are taken off and placed inside for courier pickup."

"Now, that is a lot better Steven. What is the name of the courier service?

"Witt Security Transport."

"How convenient. Steven you remember where in the city Witt Security Transport is located?"

"Market Point Avenue, Long island City."

"Good boy Steven, now you rest and relax and enjoy my hospitality."

Locking Steven back in the room. Rosario made a phone call.

"Get a watch on Witt Transport Security, Hunters Point Ave, Long Island, City. Photograph all their trucks and I want it in my hands tomorrow."

CHAPTER SIXTY-SIX

102nd Squad
1962

Sean took the call.

"Detective Feeney 102nd Squad."

"Detective, this is Barney Vickers. You told me to call you if Rosario contacted me, well he did today."

"What did he want?"

"He needs me and few drivers for a job. Wants me to meet him two days from today at a garage at Bay 7th and Bath Avenue. I told him I would show with the drivers."

"That's good Barney, do whatever he wants, we'll make sure you come out okay."

Barney hung up. Sean went over to Red.

"Barney Vickers got a call from Rosario. Whatever is going down happens two days from today."

They went to see Lou and tell him what Rosario was planning.

"You spoke to the father, did he have any idea what Steven might be telling Rosario?"

"All he told us was besides Dynex and VBS the son had worked in Wyoming, Venezuela, and the Netherlands spending time at those subsidiaries." said Red.

Then Red became silent and was looking out the window. Lou looked at Sean and said,

"What's the matter with him now?"

"He's thinking, give him a minute." said Sean.

Red came out of his trance and looked at Sean.

"We have to go back and question the father about the Netherlands right now. Lou I'll have the answer to your question when we get back."

"I will wait with bated breath Detective Blackman."

They caught up with Harvey Witt at his club on 58th and Madison Avenue.

"Mr. Witt, we need to know about your Netherlands subsidiary?

'That's a diamond house in Amsterdam. Company is Baron Incorporated."

Red queried,

"Mr. Witt, does Baron distribute from Amsterdam?"

Witt thought for a few seconds,

"No, Baron has an office on W. 47th Street, and all distribution is from there."

"How do the diamonds come to the states?"

"Every Wednesday a special flight arrives at Idlewild, and an armed courier brings the package to 47th Street."

Sean looked at Red and said,

"That is what they are going hit. Wednesday is two days from now." Red nodded yes.

"Mr. Witt please give Detective Feeney every detail about the incoming shipment. Excuse me I have to make a phone call."

Red found a phone and dialed the Squad. Joe Williams picked up and he asked for the Lou.

"Casey."

"Boss, they are going to grab a shipment of diamonds coming in from Amsterdam. Witt Corporation has a subsidiary on 47th Street. The shipment arrives at Idlewild two days from today.

"Wow, we haven 't got much time. Good work Red, what else do you need?"

"I need a home address for Johnny Rosario, how fast can. you get it?"

Stay on the line, a few minutes. Red watched Sean taking notes as Witt talked about the diamond operation. Five minutes went by, then Lou came back on.

"Red, Rosario has a house at 471 Carolina Road, Douglaston, Queens."

"Lou, we're almost finished here. Sean and I are going to Rosario's house to view the action. I got a feeling on this one."

"Ok kid, so far your feelings have been good."

They finished with Harvey Witt and drove to the address in Douglaston. Setting up on the street they observed three cars in the driveway. Running the plates, two of the cars were registered to East New York Distribution Associates, the other was registered to Rosario's wife. A black Lincoln pulled into the driveway. At that moment the front door of the house opened and a woman with two children came out. The driver of the Lincoln got out and opened the rear passenger door. A single man in an expensive suit exited. He was rushed by the two kids, whom he picked up. The wife came over and kissed him.

A few minutes went by and the woman and children got into the car registered to Rosario's wife.

"Now we know who Mrs. Rosario is" said Sean.

"And the way the kids hugged him, that's Johnny" said Red.

The wife backed out of the driveway. Johnny and his driver did not enter thru the front door but went to a side door off the driveway.

Red started up the car.

"Why are you leaving, Rosario is in his house, aren't we going to trail him?" asked Sean.

"Don't have to, I've seen enough. We need to meet with Lou and the Squad."

CHAPTER SIXTY-SEVEN

102nd Squad
1962

The small conference room was packed. Lt. Casey sat down at the head of the table. To his right was Sgt. Crandall and the rest of the seats were Joe Williams, Gus Antaknockis, Sean and Red.

Lou says,

"This case regarding Steven Witt has now entered a final phase. The work done by Bagels and Beer has been outstanding. In my time as your Lou, this present squad of detectives is the best. I'm going to turn over this final phase to Red Blackman."

Red stated,

"This is what we know so far. Steven Witt is back in the country and is most likely being held by Johnny Rosario for information on a new job. We know from Barney Vickers something is going down two days from now. According to Harvey Witt, Steven was trained at the following Witt Corporation locales;

Venezuela's Lake Maracaibo oil fields, Rawlins, Wyoming natural gas fields and Amsterdam, Netherlands Baron International offices. My partner and I have concluded that the most likely plan would be the diamonds of Baron International. The connection between Amsterdam and New York is that every Wednesday at 6AM a large shipment of diamonds arrive at Idlewild destined for Baron International at 158 W. 47th Street. Wednesday is two days from today."

Everyone in the room moved in their chairs. Sean took over.

"At 6AM the weekly private flight from Amsterdam arrives at Idlewild and taxis over to the TWA Cargo Facility, where the shipment is held for the arrival of a Witt Transport Security vehicle. Witt Transport will pick up the shipment and from Idlewild will go to the W. 47th offices of Baron. Somewhere along this route, Rosario and company will make its move. Red and I learned from Harvey Witt the route of the courier vehicle; From TWA Cargo to the Van Wyk to the Long Island Expressway, to the Queens Expressway to the Queens Midtown Tunnel. We expect the courier vehicle will be taken down inside the Queens Midtown Tunnel."

"Why do it in the tunnel and not on the expressways? Asked Gus.

Red answered.

"Vehicles going too fast for them to set up. What slower place in the world than the Queens Midtown with Christmas eight days away. We expect blocking vehicles at both ends, they will hit the courier inside the tunnel and come out in another vehicle. Their block vehicles will let them out of the tunnel, then they are free in Manhattan with a lot of bridges and tunnels to go wherever they want. Unpredictable has been the key to their operations. The television heist in Delaware was started by setting off false security alarms to the point the cops slowed down their response. We are banking on them doing something unpredictable.

"Red, so they get out of the tunnel where do you stop them?" asked Sgt. Crandall.

"Once out of the tunnel you go with main traffic flow, and that ends at 2nd Avenue below 37th Street. We stop them there"

"I like it, makes sense." Said Joe.

"Red, tell us the specifics, where we station our personnel and units?" inquired Lou.

"Joe will be at TWC Cargo. He will identify the courier vehicle, then follow it to the Queens Expressway. He will hand over to Gus. Joe, you pull ahead and pass the courier full speed and beat it into the tunnel and wait for the perps vehicle to exit. Gus will follow the bumper of the courier into the tunnel. Gus you are to identify the blockers as you enter the tunnel. In the tunnel the perps car will be right behind the blockers, this where you ID the car. Once they have the package, the perps car will be the only car exiting, but Lou we are still going to need eyes inside the tunnel, two uniforms with radios should do. Not to get involved, just stand on the catwalks and identify the make, model and color. Once outside Joe you follow the perp vehicle. Lou, Joe will need an ESU truck to back him up. Everything will end at 2nd Avenue where Sgt. Crandall, Sean and I will be waiting with another ESU truck. We are going to need 2nd Avenue going south blocked at 37th Street. That's the way we envision it going down in Manhattan. While this is in motion, Lou and the DEA hit East New York Distribution Associates with a search warrant. Place should be loaded with Centro and Television sets. Sandy Malkin will be wishing he was back in Russia Additionally, Bernie Rodriquez and the FBI will hit Rosario's house in Douglaston."

"What the hell is at his house? asked Joe.

"Steven Witt of course."

"Now how do you know that?" asked Lou.

"Sean and I surveilled the house when Rosario came home. There were three cars in the driveway. One was registered to his wife, the other two were registered to East New York Distribution. When Rosario got out of the car, the wife and kids came out of the front door to greet him. The wife and kids then left in her car Rosario goes to the side door facing the driveway, not the front door. Once inside he can go to the basement, and that is where Steven is being kept."

Gus looked at Joe and they smiled as they shook their heads, Sean smiled. Lou looked at the Sergeant and said.

"He represents the future, you and I are dinosaurs.

"Does anyone have questions? asked Red.

"I do" said Sean.

"Yes, go ahead partner."

"Can you repeat that over again, I got lost in the tunnel."

The room exploded in laughter.

CHAPTER SIXTY-EIGHT

Café Odessa
1962

Sandy Malkin welcomed Rosario with a hug, and the Russian kiss on both cheeks.

"Are you ready for the job tomorrow?"

"Yes, it will all go well."

"How much are we looking at?"

"My houseguest said $85 million was the smallest he ever saw. We may get more."

"Once you get it back to the warehouse, I'll be there with my appraiser who will tell us the full value.

You'll get your percentage right there." said Malkin.

"Good, the quicker the better."

"Johnny, your houseguest does he have any more jobs for us?"

"The only thing he mentioned of any worth was his father's house. Maybe three million in jewels, not much compared to what he has given us."

"Well, I think it is time we say goodbye to Mr. Steven Witt, kill him."

"I will Mr. Malkin right after we complete this job, if that is alright with you?"

"Of course, Johnny, business first."

CHAPTER SIXTY-NINE

Diamond Heist
1962

5:00 AM Wednesday Joe Williams sat inside TWA Cargo facility. From the inside he had clear view of runway 23 East. The head of Security came by with a cup of coffee and told him the flight was on time. At 6:00 AM he looked out and saw an all-white two engine jet land. At 6:05 AM Tail # PH1007 stopped and two persons exited the plane. They came into the receiving area and paperwork was exchanged. The two people returned to the plane, which was getting refueled. The package, about the size of a toolbox, was placed in a locked fenced-in area. At 06:45 AM a white and red GMC 3500 armored truck pulled up to the facility. The signage on the side said, 'Witt Security Transport'. Two armed men exited and came into the receiving area. The package was removed from the secure area and handed over to the truck guards. As the truck pulled out, Joe Williams trailed behind. Onto the Van Wyk, then to the Long Island Expressway West. Joe got on the radio.

"K10 to K19"

"K19 to K10 go"

"On LIE-west now, what is your milepost?"

"Milepost 23W"

"10-4"

Gus was waiting at the milepost in a red pickup truck, an American flag fluttered from its antenna.

"K10 to K19 one mile from your location."

"10-4"

Gus started up and got in the slow lane and waited. The white and red armored sped by followed by Joe. He got up to speed and got behind Joe, flashed his lights and Joe pulled out and sped ahead of the armored truck. For the next ten minutes Gus was maybe a car length behind the armored truck.

The morning traffic was on and Joe made it thru the toll, as he exited the tunnel he pulled over and waited. As the truck entered the tolls the traffic into the tunnel started to slow. Gus remained behind the truck. The armored truck entered the two lanes going into Manhattan, it was in the right lane behind a tractor trailer truck. Gus maintained his position and noticed another tractor trailer in the left lane staying even with the other tractor trailer. He radioed.

"K19 to K10 we are behind two tractor trailers, this looks like it is going down."

Joe responded, "10-4"

Then Gus came on,

"K19 to K10 we are dead stopped. Trailer to my left is moving up, a black Lincoln has moved parallel to the truck. Trailer on left has stopped. Jesus, they are firing at the truck tires, truck is stopped! Three perps getting out with guns and whatlooks like a gas gun. Oh boy, they fired into the vehicle! It is smoking. Guards coming out, they knocked them out, one going into truck, came out with package. Leaving in Black Lincoln NY LZD-34Q. Repeat Black Lincoln LZD-34Q. Trailer on left has moved to right lane, Lincoln is moving. Will take care of trailers. Out.

In the middle of the tunnel a uniformed officer on a catwalk saw the moving Lincoln and radioed it in.

Gus with gun drawn ran up to the trailer and opened the driver's door, he yanked the guy from his seat to the tunnel pavement.

"What's your name asshole?"

"Bobby Hoffman"

He cuffed him and went to the next trailer. Yanking the door open, he found the driver with his hands up.

He aimed his gun at the driver and asked.

"What's your name?"

"Barney Vickers."

"Ok, your safe. I'm going to handcuff you, just sit here. They will put you in a patrol car and take you home."

"Thank you."

Joe saw the speeding Lincoln exit the tunnel and he took off after it. As he passed an intersecting street, he saw an Emergency Services Unit pull in behind him. The Lincoln was moving at a steady rate toward Second Avenue. As the Lincoln came off a slight curve it saw two police trucks blocking the road and two unmarked cars in front of the trucks. Sgt. Crandall had a twelve-gauge pump shotgun aimed at the front tires, he fired and both tires exploded. The car came to a complete stop. Behind it the ESU truck and Joe had blocked it in. Two minutes went by the driver's door opened and he started firing to the front. The front passenger door opened, and he fired towards the rear. Both men were taken down by ESU marksmen. There was a silence for about a minute. When the right rear door opened and a man came up with a gun which he dropped on the ground and raised his hands and yelling,

"Don't kill me! Don't kill me!

Red yelled to him.

"Keep walking forward with your hands up. Keep walking forward."

He started to walk, when there was shot from inside the car and man fell dead on his face.

Red got mad and looked at Sean.

"Rosario never sees the inside of a courtroom, got that."

Sean nodded.

The left rear passenger door opened. Out stepped Johnny Rosario. He was holding a package in one hand and in the other he had sub-machine gun. He yelled,

"Fuck you bastards!"

Raising the sub-machine gun toward Red he took aim. Sean held his .357 Magnum and sighted him in, he fired and hit Rosario dead center between the eyes. Red watched as Rosario crumpled to the ground.

Meanwhile at the East New York Distribution Associates warehouse seven teams of armed DEA agents accompanied by ESU units broke down the doors. They found what they were looking for, Centro and TV's. When Lt. Casey came inside, he saw fifteen men all against the wall. What caught his interest was one of them was well dressed. He went over behind this person and said,

"Sandy Malkin our prisons are not as bad as the ones in Russia, but you will be there till you die. Just tell your lawyer these are Federal charges, and even though you think you're a good American citizen it is not going to help."

Lou walked away smiling.

And at 471 Carolina Road, Douglaston, Queens the FBI team of ten agents hit the front door.

A screaming Mrs. Rosario holding her two children then began to scream and cry. Agents came in through the side driveway door and went down into the basement. One of

Johnny's men drew his gun and was killed instantly, the other one begged for his life. They opened the locked room and found Steven lying prone on the floor. He was alive. Special Agent Bernie Rodriquez had him stand up and said,

"Steven Witt you are under arrest for aiding and abetting a criminal enterprise. Cuff him and book him with that other guy."

Two hours later Steven got his telephone call. Instead of calling a lawyer he called his father.

Harvey Witt answered and heard his son's voice, then he hung up.

CHAPTER SEVENTY

102nd Squad
1963

Christmas and New Year's had come and gone. All the accolades over the last case had ended. The department and its brass considered the squad an exceptional group and went by the old adage, if it's not broke don't fix it. However, with time things change. Lt. Casey turned in his retirement papers. He and his wife had plans, and now was the right time. An exceptional leader and man who had completed his service honorably. His replacement was a no brainer. Byron Crandall would become Lou, while Joe Williams took over the squad Sergeant role. Gus Antaknockis was now the senior Detective 1st Grade and rightfully so. Each of these men were unique in their own ways. They had all learned the ways and means of the job, the department, and the Street.

On a slow day Crandall picked up his phone and made a call. It was answered by a sweet female voice.

"Is that little brother of mine treating my beautiful baby sister, right? If not, tell him the big brother teddy bear is coming to make it right."

They both laughed and had a great conversation and planned to meet for lunch.

Gus was sitting at his desk looking at a photo of his family. He had known his wife Sophia since he was eleven years old and twenty-three years of marriage were wonderful. His three kids Nick, Bobby and Athena were his greatest achievement. What a lucky man am I he thought. The phone rang it was Sophia,

"Gus, you busy?"

"No, what's the matter, everything alright?"

"Yes, everything is ok, here Nick wants to speak to you."

"Hello Dad."

"Yes, Nick, what do you need?"

"Nothing, I just want to let you know."

"Know what?"

"I got a letter today from our Congressman Joseph Garber. He has appointed me to report to the United States Naval Academy this August. Pretty good news Dad. Dad? Dad you there?"

There was silence on Gus's end, for he was crying tears of joy.

Marci Baxter and Joe Williams had taken a weekend trip to Cape Cod. It was early before the busy season started. The motel was right on the beach, so they walked the barren seashore as the sun set. He proposed to her on the beach. She said yes, cried and kissed her man. Joe could not live without her for her beauty was internal as well as external, and most important they were in love with each other. He knew from the first time he saw her she was the one.

Sean and Red were rewarded by getting a second telephone for their desk. Both were put in for awards that would take a while, due to the bureaucracy. However, due to the insistence of Lt. Casey they were both promoted to Detective 2nd Grade. Red took full advantage of programs opened for NYPD Detectives, like the FBI National Training Academy and a new forensics course called DNA Evidence. Sean saw the light and enrolled in classes at John Jay, he wanted a college degree. Bagels and Beer had made a name for themselves. They were truly partners made for each other. And that reputation would eventually become legend.

www.ingramcontent.com/pod-product-compliance
Lightning Source LLC
LaVergne TN
LVHW040133080526
838202LV00042B/2892